Out of Mind

Michael Burke

Parlor Press
Anderson, South Carolina
www.parlorpress.com

Parlor Press LLC, Anderson, South Carolina, USA

S A N: 2 5 4 - 8 8 7 9

  Library of Congress Cataloging-in-Publication Data

Burke, Michael, 1939-
  Out of mind / Michael Burke. -- First edition.
    pages cm.
  ISBN 978-1-60235-598-9 (pbk. : acid-free paper)
  1. Private investigators--Fiction. 2. Mystery fiction. 3.
Noir fiction. I. Title.
  PS3602.U75525O97 2014
  813'.6--dc23

                                        2014035725

Cover design by Tom Chapin and Michael Burke.
Printed on acid-free paper.

2 3 4 5
First Edition

Parlor Press, LLC is an independent publisher of
scholarly and trade titles in print and multimedia
formats. This book is available in paper and digital
formats from Parlor Press on the World Wide Web at
http://www.parlorpress.com or through online and brick-
and-mortar bookstores. For submission information or to
find out about Parlor Press publications, write to Parlor
Press, 3015 Brackenberry Drive, Anderson, SC 29621, or
e-mail editor@parlorpress.com.

Praise for *Music of the Spheres*

"Burke once again smoothly blends allusions to Greek mythology with familiar detective fiction tropes in his second mystery featuring winning, if slightly dim, PI Johnny "Blue" Heron (after 2009's *Swan Dive*). When Heron learns that Hank Menotti, who was convicted of manslaughter after stabbing his father, George Windsore, to death 12 years earlier, has been released from the state pen, Heron drives over to the house of George's son and Hank's half-brother, Billy, in the unnamed Northeastern town that serves as the series' setting. There he finds Billy dying with a knife wound in his back. Enlisted to assist in the murder investigation, Heron seizes the chance to rekindle his relationship with his ex-girlfriend and newly appointed chief of police, Kathy McGregor. Those who like their noir with a touch of whimsical humor will be satisfied."
—*Publisher's Weekly* (2009)

Praise for *Swan Dive*

"Move over, Dashiell Hammett. Make room, Cornell Woolrich. With his first novel, *Swan Dive*, Michael Burke joins the pantheon of private eye muses. This fast-paced who-done-it is a masterful achievement of unpredictable narrative cast with diverse and engaging characters. Michael Burke spices his tale with an artist's eye and philosopher's wit as he enlightens and entertains."
—Sidney Offit

"Where has Michael Burke been hiding? His first book, a detective thriller called *Swan Dive*, has the speed and sex of Spillane, the plotting of Chandler and the wit and charm of Hammett. There's money, murder, and mayham and, to keep things bubbling, a bevy of gorgeous women—the most tempting and intriguing of whom may just be Leda and the Swan! I couldn't put it down.
—John Gruen

". . . I could well afford to smile while silently concealed in my mystery."

—Ralph Ellison, *Invisible Man*

Out of Mind

1

IT WAS A HOT, DAMP AUGUST NIGHT, and the Perseids were spectacular. The asphalt plant next door had closed a month ago, and a steady breeze carried the summer haze away to the ocean, allowing our stars to shine brightly in a pitch-black sky. The moon was visiting Australia and didn't inter-fere. I sat on a deck chair on the fire escape sipping a martini, watching the meteors streak away from the torso of Perseus. A few spectacular beauties stole the show. The Swift-Tuttle comet had swept through our solar system some years ago and left a trail of dust for the earth to plow through every August. He'll be back in a hundred and thirty years to replenish the supply.

The Perseids are the finest shower of the year, although it seems a bit callous to eagerly watch for the meteors, chunks of rock and iron that had been traveling for millions of years, to meet their fate. Each creates a glowing trail that shines majes-tically for an instant before it disintegrates into nothingness. Maybe we'd all like to go down in a blaze of glory, or maybe I'm just feeling low because Kathy turned me down again. Po-lice Chief Kathy MacGregor has something else, or someone else, on her mind these days. Told me to get a job. She's right. I need something to do. I should reopen my office. The sign could read:

Or, I could run an ad in *The Daily Flyer:*

> Got a problem.
> Want to spy on someone
> Call Blue at . . .

I'd fallen asleep, the sun had risen, and my cell phone interrupted my dreams with its version of Ride of the Valkyries. I climbed back in through the window, found it on top of the microwave in the kitchen, and flipped it open, "Good morning."

"Good afternoon." A female voice greeted me. "Is this Mr. Heron?"

"Yes, ma'am." I checked my watch.

"I was told you are a good investigator. I may need one. Are you interested?"

"So far, yes." I had some old friends in town who tended to give me good referrals.

"Can we meet? Where's your office?"

'Well. We're in the middle of renovations at the moment, new paint, might even put in a new desk. I could come by your place."

"No," she answered. "I'd rather not be seen talking with you. My husband might come home. Can you suggest somewhere discreet?"

I thought for a second. "There's a bar right off City Hall Park, not far from Police Headquarters. It has a small sign out front, LEROY'S BAR AND STRIP CLUB. He likes to keep a low profile. You know the place?"

"No. Is it private?"

"On the northwest corner of the Park. You can't miss it. There's lot behind the bar where you can leave your car. If we meet there in the morning, I doubt you will see any of your friends."

"Eleven o'clock tomorrow, then." She was about to hang up.

"Could I have a name?"

She hesitated, then offered her name, "Louella. But you must keep this case totally confidential. Don't tell a soul."

"I'm good at confidential—it's my business." In this case confidential would be easy—all I know about it is one name, Louella."

"See you then, Mr. Heron. And," she added, "good luck with the renovation."

2

Monday Morning, and I'm driving down West Main Street in my old BMW, my rusty Beamer, headed for the center of town to meet a woman named Louella. If experience serves me well, she will hire me to check up on her husband. She will have a reason, maybe real, maybe a fantasy, to suspect that he is cheating on her. A phone call that went dead when she answered; her husband working late; a letter he reads and says it's nothing and won't show it to her; a pair of panties in his pocket that aren't hers. Mostly these are the results of his stupidity, or a sign that he really wants her to find out but he hasn't admitted that to himself.

Louella asked me to choose a place to meet, where she wouldn't be recognized. I find myself standing on the edge of City Hall Park in front of LeRoy's Bar and Strip Club. I suspected that she was wealthy, so I picked a spot where there's no chance she will meet anyone who knows her. No one from her side of the tracks is going to be found at LeRoy's, especially at eleven o'clock in the morning. I push through the door, as I've done a thousand times before, and step into LeRoy's artificial world. The bar slowly comes into view as my eyes adjust to the dark. Small tables are scattered randomly around the room, each with three or four wooden chairs. The bar at the far side is backed by a huge mirror papered over with signed photos and ads for drink specials that don't exist anymore. Whoever heard of a Freddie Fudpucker? LeRoy is behind the bar, the old hippie, white hair pulled into a ponytail, a quiet face and dark eyes that don't miss a thing. I've known LeRoy for years. There are a few regulars glued to bar stools and a guilty couple hunched over one of the tables. A lone figure sat at a table in the back, a glass of wine untouched before her. I feel her eyes on me as I approach.

LeRoy looks toward me. A quick shake of my head tells him not to recognize me. I don't want the usual greeting: "Hey Blue, what's up? One martini on the way." My new employer might draw the wrong conclusion.

LeRoy turned back to the guys at the bar, but I knew he'd be keeping track of my every move. I'll have to give him a good story tomorrow: "LeRoy, you know that rich chick I met the other day? Those diamond studs that pierced her ears, the ones you couldn't see were even bigger."

"Good morning. Are you John Heron?" She spoke slowly.

Louella stood up and held out her hand. She was tall, thin, and pretty; her body clutched by a tight black suit. Straight black hair, precisely drawn eyebrows arched over eyes that looked inside my brain. She was a bit older than I was, but any telltale sags or wrinkles had been sent away; her skin was stretched so tightly that if she had tripped, she would have shattered into tiny pieces. She was poised, elegant, and obviously wealthy. She could have sold the labels off her dress for the price of my car, and I knew the diamonds in her earrings weren't imposters.

Her hand took mine with a confident grip, and we sat opposite each other at the small table.

"Good morning, Louella. What can I do for you?"

"It's Louella Lafonte." We sat quietly; she looked me over and then asked, "Have you done cases like this before, Mr. Heron? Where a wife needs to find out if her husband is unfaithful?"

"Actually, that's pretty much all us private eyes are good for—that and consuming large quantities of alcohol."

Louella didn't smile. "Then you may need a drink?" She waved at LeRoy with a gesture that dared him to ignore her. He slipped out from behind the bar, wiped his hands on his apron, and stood by the table. "A Chardonnay, perhaps?" LeRoy asked me through a poorly hidden grin.

"A martini, if you could. Bombay Sapphire, on the rocks, with a twist."

"Really," LeRoy said, and turned to go.

"And make that dry, as dry as the eyes of . . ."

" . . . the eyes of the devil's pallbearers." LeRoy finished my sentence for me and left for the bar.

"Mrs. Lafonte. What can you tell me?"

"Not much. I want you to find out if he's playing around," Louella said as though my need for details was irrelevant.

"Could you give his me his name and where you, or he, live and work?"

Louella leaned back with an impatient look. She needed some encouragement. I picked up the martini that had appeared on the table and raised it for a toast. We clinked glasses and she raised hers, hesitated a second, and then drained it as though she had just crawled out of Death Valley. I then learned that she was married to Mr. Lawrence Lafonte. He was a respected member of the community, the face of a few upstanding community organizations. He was the kind voice behind a charity named KittyLuv, which occupied an old building on the southwestern edge of the town square. Our town was proud of KittyLuv—after all they had something to do with kittens. I never knew exactly what they did, probably because I harbored a deep-seated ignorance of anything that had to do with cats.

Louella told me that she and Lawrence lived in Marble Hill, the ritzy area on the edge of town that produced most of my clients. She slid a business card out of a slick leather purse and handed it to me.

"You wouldn't have a photograph of your husband, by any chance?" I asked.

"This should help." Louella held out a slick brochure. The front featured a picture of a distinguished-looking gentleman posing before a giant picture of a smiling kitten, or was it frowning? Large fuzzy letters announced KITTYLUV.

"And you can look up KittyLuv on the web. You'll find Larry's face all over the site."

"One other thing before you go. Do you have a directory of the KittyLuv staff? It would help me run down prospective suitors."

"No, but there's one on their website." Louella thought for a moment. "You'll need a name and password to get that."

"You'll have to trust me a bit, Mrs. Lafonte. I'll need to follow your husband's schedule, where he goes, who he hangs with. Affairs have a way of advertizing themselves, if watched closely."

Louella hesitated, then agreed. "Okay, here." She wrote on the back of the brochure. "My e-mail name and password. It'll get you on to the private section of the website. It's not too interesting, but you can find names, addresses, phone numbers, and some meeting notes, that kind of thing. I doubt you'll need it."

"Your husband is there every day?"

"Most weekdays and Saturdays, although he does travel a lot for fund-raising events. Sometimes he takes the late train to the city to meet his accountant. He doesn't usually get home until quite late, or sometimes stays over." Louella paused, as if it just occurred to her that spending the night in the city might seem a bit suspicious. She added, "I really don't keep track of all his fundraising; it's really pretty boring." It sounded like Louella and I shared an opinion about kittens.

"What makes you think he is having an affair?" It was a question that had been hanging in the air since we met.

She looked me in the eye. "A woman can tell. He keeps strange hours, doesn't come home until late, not interested in making love, the usual." Louella pushed her chair back and stood up, but I pressed for more details.

"You probably have some suspicion about who the lady is—that might give me somewhere to start."

"Lady! Are you kidding?" Louella's face turned red. " That floozy little redhead who pretends to be his assistant. What's her name? Vera. Vera something. Vera Booby is what she should be called." She turned to leave.

"Would you like to know what I charge?" I thought I should bring the subject up.

Louella looked somewhat surprised, as though she couldn't be bothered with such details. "Yes. What do you charge?"

$500 a day plus expenses."

"Okay," she shrugged.

Obviously I should have said $1,000 a day, plus expenses, health care, and a retirement fund—or perhaps included some more personal services.

Louella took one step toward the door but then turned back, "One more thing, Mr. Heron. All I want you to do is find one solid piece of evidence, proof of an affair. Nothing else. And everything you learn is for me alone. You do understand me?"

"Understood."

The few patrons in the bar watched her cross to the door and disappear into the glare of sunlight that burst in from the outside. She had carved a path through the room that lingered on after she was gone. If Larry was having an affair, it wouldn't be hard to track it down. But the puzzle that intrigued me was Louella. What would she do with the info? Was she after money? Did she want an excuse to leave her husband? Would she plan revenge? Louella didn't realize that her life would also come under scrutiny. She was a woman who was not happy with her world. I recognized her predicament. I was trying to leave a world behind and she was trying to find one.

She hadn't offered to pay the tab, a sure sign of wealth. I could consider the cost of the drinks as work expenses, but it probably wouldn't be ethical to charge her for the second martini that LeRoy was already mixing for me.

3

Louella Lafonte left me sitting at a table in the back of the room at LeRoy's. I carried my half-finished martini to the end of the bar, where I could sit with my back to the wall and enjoy a view down a length of the polished mahogany. Midday was a quiet time, and LeRoy didn't need help to serve the customers at the bar and those seated at the tables. The drinking crowd wouldn't descend on the place until later. He was good at his job, but the only place the aging hippie with a long graying ponytail was really comfortable was behind the bar. Get him out in the open and he was a product of a different time—a Woodstock holdover, one of those guys who spent his younger days smoking pot at peace marches. He was a good confidante however, as bartenders should be, and I could share almost any secret with him. He dried his hands on a towel and tossed it under the bar.

"So Blue, she looked much too fancy for you. Talk her out of one of those diamonds and you could finally trade in that rusty old Beamer of yours."

"That's true, though I still ended up paying for the drinks. But," I added, "I got a job."

"Congratulations. Who do you have to shoot?"

"Can't tell you—professional ethics and all. But I do need to use your computer."

"Be my guest. You know where it is. The office door's open."

I spent the next half hour in LeRoy's small office logged on to the KittyLuv site. There were pictures of kittens, of course, and also a mission statement, a motto—'A home for every kitten'—testimonials, success stories, and the many opportunities to make a donation. KittyLuv was a charitable organization devoted to improving the lives of cute kittens. Volunteers would find abandoned kittens, and KittyLuv would place them into loving homes. Kittens all over the world qualified for this service, and the site displayed before and after pictures from Europe, South America, and Canada. The before picture would show a scraggly little creature huddling behind a garbage can. In the after, the same kitten was clean and trimmed, snuggled happily into someone's lap. Each kitten had a name and a story. For a small donation the cute little fellow would send you a personal thank you note. There was a chronology of past and future events and fundraisers, which Mr. Lafonte presided over. A few were in town, and at a couple of nearby high schools and colleges, but the biggest were in Boston, New York, and Philadelphia. Louella Lafonte's e-mail and password allowed me access to the site's private area. I printed out a list of the office personnel: names, phone numbers, job titles, and a staff photo.

Back on my stool at the end of the bar, I asked LeRoy, "You know that KittyLuv outfit?"

"Of course. They're just across the Park from here."

"Do you know anybody there? Maybe some come in now and then to wash away the taste of cat hair."

"A few drop by, but I don't know the names, except for Samson, the chauffeur. He's here quite a bit, and sometimes hits the strip club downstairs. I think he's quite the ladies' man."

"Can you describe him?"

"Tall, handsome, long sandy hair, nice smile."

I looked at the personnel list. "There's a Samuel Wheatley, listed as chauffeur, must be him."

"Probably—but he can be a problem. Get a few drinks in him and he gets rowdy. Once, I had to throw him out. He didn't like that much."

"But he still comes back."

"Yeah. I don't think he can resist the strippers."

"How about the security guy, name's Fitzhugh Botsby believe it or not. Does he come by?"

"No. Don't know him. Some of the girls came by last week for a birthday party; some really cute gals, but I don't know their names. Why do you ask?"

"My new boss wants me to do a little research—can't say what—but I'm going to have to learn a bit about kittens."

"Are you sure they hired the right guy?" LeRoy laughed as he walked away to attend to a blue-suited gentleman who wanted to get a head start on his drinking day.

I studied the list. Lawrence Lafonte was President. Three women were listed as his assistants: Sybil Troy, Rose Christensen, and Betty Whalen. A Vera Bishop was listed under accounting, along with Marcus Doolittle and Thalia Davidson. The office consisted of Mr. Lafonte, eight women and two men, and the chauffeur and security guy. The staff photos didn't include Samson and Fitzhugh. There was a beaming Lawrence Lafonte surrounded by a bevy of beautiful women. I looked for Vera's accounting coworkers and found Thalia, and I figured the bald guy in the back was Marcus Doolittle. It was time for me to take a look at their headquarters.

My eyes had adjusted to the dim interior light, and when I stepped out on the street, I was blinded by the brilliant August sun. I walked right into a policeman, knocking him against the wall.

"Well, Mr. Heron. I didn't expect to bump into you this early in the day."

The policeman was a policewoman, Kathy, Kathy Mac-Gregor, Chief of Police. She was dressed in full uniform, her soft brown hair spilling out from under the billed cap and the brass buttons on her chest pressing forward to scatter beams of sunlight like cut diamonds. You'd think her looks would have exempted her from the position of Chief.

"Kathy, how are you?" I smiled.

"Fine," she answered stiffly.

"Why so formal, Kathy my love? When am I going to see you?"

"You're seeing me now." The August heat was not melting the ice.

"How about Friday? We could have a nice dinner, go over to The Swan, see the show, and then spend the night together. Like old times."

"Blue, I have to tell you something."

I waited.

"At the Police conference last month. I met someone there."

"Okay, so you met another nice policewoman. That's fine, as long as we can get together for a threesome now and then."

"Blue, you're impossible!" Kathy sighed. "I met a guy."

"A guy?"

"Yes, he's nice, he's handsome, he's smart, and he has a fucking job." Kathy was angry.

"He has a fucking job?"

"Yes! He has a *fucking* job!" Kathy said loudly enough to cause two passersby to turn their heads. "A job, you know, he has a life!"

"I'm working now," I protested.

"Yes, for the next week, if you're lucky. Then it's back to the Dung Hill Arms, drinking martinis, and watching the rail yards decay." She turned and walked away. I thought I saw her wipe a tear from her eye, but that wouldn't be the Kathy I knew.

"Bye." I said quietly. "See you soon." The Police Department was a nondescript building a half block away, next to the grand columned Courthouse. I watched Kathy walk by the two squad cars parked in front and disappear through the revolving door.

4

City Hall Park was a quiet oasis in the center of town, framed by most of the town's administration: the Courthouse, Police Headquarters, and the Mayor Montgomery Office Building. A grand red oak grew in the center and provided welcome shade that shifted during the day with the angle of the sun. The benches across the street from City Hall were filled with the lunch crowd. I picked up a hot dog from the vendor at the corner covered with mustard and sauerkraut. The Park sloped down to the southeastern edge where the KittyLuv building was located. The only bench that overlooked that corner was inhabited by one of the Park's semi-permanent residents, a bearded, graying man wearing an ancient, frayed serge suit, so oversized that it masked any evidence of his real shape. He wore a wide gold-and-blue striped tie that was chic in the fifties, and that doubled as a napkin. A strange unidentifiable aroma formed an almost visible cloud that hovered over him and added an exotic flavor to my lunch. Our town's enforcers of moral cleanliness had tried many times to send him on his way, but he persevered and eventually they gave up. He was categorized on the police blotter as Male Loiterer Number Six, and 'Number Six' stuck as his name. He had gained a moment of notoriety when the local paper included him in an article about the decline of our morals, and then they forgot about him. I sat down beside Number Six, and gave him a brief "Hello." He didn't say anything, or even look my way; he was concentrating on the scene before him.

KittyLuv was headquartered in a classic nineteenth-century building, an elegant relic from the past. Four stories high but only as wide as a two-car garage. A marble arch framed the large, wooden double door at the entrance, and each of the floors above sported an ornate balcony. A massive American flag waved from a rod jutting out just below the peaked roof. A driveway led alongside the left wall of the building, then sloped down to a parking lot in back. A long black limousine sat at the curb in front of the building; a uniformed chauffeur—two rows of brass buttons, slick gloves, and a cap tilted confidently to one side—leaned against the front fender nursing a cigarette. Must be Samson.

KittyLuv's staff was returning after their lunch break. Number Six suddenly sat upright, his interest aroused, and stared straight ahead.

I tried again. "Nice day, don't ya think?"

No answer.

"Nice car," I tried again, motioning toward the limousine. Silence.

"Too nice!" Number Six suddenly growled. "Too damn nice!"

We sat for a while watching the people on the sidewalk come and go.

"Give money for kittens and look what they buy. What fucking kitten is that going to help?"

"Their brochure says they do good things." I held out the brochure that Louella had given me.

"Where'd you get that?" Six finally turned toward me.

"It's their public face. Apparently they give money to rescue homeless kittens in Africa and find them nice loving places to stay."

"Yeah! Some cuddly, little, fucking home. Fat chance!"

"There's pictures, look." I opened the pamphlet to a picture of an adorable kitten, tenderly held by a young woman. "They saved this little kitten from a life of misery and loneliness. Just for, like, twenty dollars or something."

"Fuck!" Number Six was getting worked up. "People gave money, and they bought that big-assed car. That's what they did!"

Number Six had a point. It wasn't really clear how the shiny limousine was helping baby cats.

"There she is." Number Six suddenly perked up.

"There who is?" I asked.

"Who asked you?" he growled and continued to stare straight ahead.

A radiant glow of red hair sat atop a figure walking toward the front door of KittyLuv. With the August sun shining, the figure was a beacon, a siren, leading the weak to their destruction. I couldn't make out her features, but I bet I'd just seen Vera Booby. Number Six had been waiting to spot her and now had fulfilled his goal for the day. He worked his way to a semi-upright position and shuffled off in the opposite direction. I called out a "see you tomorrow" and watched him shrink into the distance. Kathy and Number Six had both abandoned me today. I envied Number Six's clear-cut vision of life. Come to the Park, wait for the red-haired vision, see her, then go off, satisfied, until tomorrow.

5

The ten-story office building was named after our ex-Mayor Norton Montgomery—no one had bothered to change its name after he went to jail. It was a mundane square brick structure, holding offices for the lawyers, accountants, and bail bondsmen that lived off the town's court system. The evenly spaced glass windows gave it the look of a ten-story chicken coop facing the park. Henry Cadman, my financial advisor, tax guy, and friend had an office on the fifth floor. The chairs in his waiting room were filled with nervous people waiting to hear about the state of their finances. A serious young woman, June Smithson, sat at a desk facing the group. She reminded me of my tenth grade math teacher, and the look on the faces of the waiting group suggested they were about to take an algebra test. She wore a conservative suit with just the right amount of jewelry, but her attempt at respectability was undermined by a whirling dervish of glowing blond hair. The out-of-control explosion rendered the rest of her attire irrelevant. I could see Henry Cadman through the glass door of his office talking seriously to a young couple. He was known to his friends as Doctor Dollar. In a room off to the side, a young fellow sat behind two large computer screens. Benny was the Doctor's assistant. He was alone.

Benny's computer skills were legendary, but his people skills were nonexistent. We always got along well, perhaps because I appreciated his eccentricities. Who else would compliment him on a yellow tie sporting a grinning clown face? I told June that I wanted to see Benny. I was first on the list to meet with him, and she sent me in.

"Hi, Benny. Nice tie."

Benny looked up, startled. "Oh, Blue. I'm sorry. I mean. Oh, that. Thanks. But you probably want to see the Doctor."

"He looks pretty busy, so if I could just leave him a message?"

"Of course, of course." Benny continued to type instructions on his computer keyboard even as he looked at me.

"There's a firm I'd like the Doctor to check into when he gets a chance." Benny's eyes lit up when I gave him the password to the KittyLuv site. He was rummaging through their inner workings before I even left the office. I suspected he really didn't need the password.

. . . .

I drove through the town on my way home. The evening traffic was light, and nearly nonexistent once I turned onto Machinist's Drive. I thought of the Drive as my own personal two-mile-long driveway, as I seldom passed anyone along the road. I crossed the narrow bridge over Hammer Creek, passed by factories that the road was built to serve but had since closed down. Iron, Inc. was running at half speed. Pharm-a-Lot still ran a pretty good business, but that was because it dealt in drugs, an industry that thrived. I passed a hulk that was slowly being absorbed by the ever-present barberry bushes and fast-growing maples. The asphalt plant next to the Arms had closed down last month; the air that blew into my apartment no longer smelled like a highway on a hot summer day. I pulled in beside the Gold Hill Arms. The Arms had begun as an elegant hotel that served the owners of the industries. It was a sturdy six-story brick building with a marble entrance and an elaborately carved frieze over the double doors. But time and a changing world had taken a toll, and the Arms was showing signs of middle age.

I parked in a spot next to the rusting van. The final two tires had gone flat, and it was slowly sinking into the soft earth. Now the Arms served as a home for transients, misfits, druggies, and deadbeats—those who were hiding from the law, breaking the law, or looking for a way to break the law. The Arms was home for those who were afraid of life, those who wished to remain invisible, and those who were trying to become invisible. The motto of the Gold Hill Arms should be carved in the marble floor of the lobby: "Out of sight—Out of mind."

I don't know why I live here—maybe it's just the observer in me. I only want to watch and listen, but an observer also needs to be invisible. I'd spent enough of my life in the spotlight, and that didn't work out so well.

Javier was our super, custodian, handyman, and doorman. He lived on the ground floor. He had converted a meeting room adjacent to the lobby into an apartment. He usually left his door open, and anyone coming through could see him settled in front of his wide-screen television set. This satisfied his duties as a doorman. As I walked through he looked up from the TV and waved.

It was a hot August night, the air was still, and my apartment was steaming. I mixed a martini and climbed out the window to the deck chair on the fire escape. The ground dropped off behind the Arms, which allowed a long view to the south. In the distance lay the railroad yards, a great expanse of tracks where locomotives used to push boxcars around, sorting out those that would sit idle from those that were linked up for trips back to the West. There was only one pusher engine still working, and most of the freight cars that remained hadn't moved in years. At the far end of the tracks I could see the lights from South Station, our main rail link to New York City. The few buildings along the edge of the tracks were dark. Only in one large stone factory did I see a glimmer of light.

6

Tuesday afternoon, sunny again, hot again, and the air was still. The sky was clear and blue—an August blue tempered by heat waves. The town was steaming, but the Park was blessed by the shadow of one cumulus cloud that sat overhead. Mother Nature was looking after Number Six. I strolled across the grass, taking advantage of the shade, and sat down on the bench next to him. He wasn't very talkative today.

I was running through plans to scope out the KittyLuv office. I could put on a tie, find a Watchtower pamphlet and become a Jehovah's Witness. But they travel in pairs, and I wasn't sure Number Six would make the grade. Maybe go in to read the gas meter, or I could conduct a poll. "Mind if I ask you a few questions about your staff—like who's sleeping with whom?" Maybe I'll just go in and ask for a massage—isn't that what KittyLuv really means? Or I could ask Hades, god of the underworld, if I could borrow his helmet, the helmet of invisibility. He never uses it anyway; it always seems to end up on someone else's head. Hermes, Athena, and Perseus used it, and it worked for them. I could slip it on, just mosey into KittyLuv and look around. I'll bet Number Six knows where to find Hades.

Something rubbed against my leg. "Go away, pussycat. Got no food."

I suppose I could go over and ask if I could help, or donate something, or volunteer for a trip to Africa to pet a kitten.

"Okay, I'll give you a scratch. But that's all, or . . ." I looked down at the cat who had decided my leg was the object of his desires. "You could help me." I picked him up; he didn't object. He thought there might be some food in the exchange. He was wearing a collar, which suggested he had wandered away from home. "Come on, pussycat. We're going for a walk. This looks like a job for KittyLuv."

Number Six finally spoke. "Name's Cat-Meow."

"Cat-Meow?"

"What'd I say?"

"Can I borrow your Cat-Meow?" I asked Number Six.

"He's not my cat," Six growled in return.

"How do you know his name is Cat-Meow?"

"Ask him."

I couldn't argue with that. I put on my sunglasses—my idea of a disguise. I cradled Cat-Meow in my arms and started down the hill. He purred happily.

Number Six called out after with his gruff voice. "Watch out for that fucker!"

I stopped. "What fucker?"

Six pointed. The long town car was waiting by the curb. The tall sandy-haired, handsome chap in full chauffeur's uniform—brass buttons and all—leaned against the front fender waiting for his riders.

I pointed at the chauffeur. "Him? He's the fucker?"

"Fucker tried to take my bench." Six spit on the ground.

"Thanks Six. I'll be careful."

The chauffeur gave me a puzzled look but didn't say anything as I passed him by and entered the building. The ground floor was an empty lobby. A sign inscribed KittyLuv pointed to the open set of stairs leading to the second floor, where I faced a long hallway. The reception area was on the right side, the door was open. It was a large, cheery office, with a large vase of flowers by the door. The three desks in the room each sported large name tags; 'Betty,' 'Sybil,' 'Rose.' Only Sybil was there. She didn't notice me at first, but I noticed her. She was quietly concentrating on the memo before her, her light dress was shifting about her thin figure as though a breeze was blowing through the room. It was hard to describe exactly what it was that made Sybil exotically beautiful. Her straight auburn hair touched her shoulders; a silver streak raced down one side. Long tempting eyelashes, light blue eye shadow, and glossy red lipstick accentuated her features and separated them from porcelain white skin. Each part of Sybil was beautiful, in and of itself, but they each went their separate ways.

"Good day, Sybil," I began.

"Hello." She looked at my lapel hoping to find a name tag.

"I'm sorry to bother you, but maybe you could help," I said with a gentle plea.

"Well, isn't he cute." Sybil rose, her dress followed, and she reached out for the happy creature in my arms. I willingly handed Cat-Meow over. Sybil snuggled him against her breast, and he rewarded me by rubbing his whiskers against her neck, pushing the dress to the side. The voyeur inside me stood at attention. I'd never appreciated the power of cats before.

"What can I do for you?" Sybil asked, directing the question either to me or Cat-Meow.

"He's not mine. I found him wandering about. I think he's homeless, so I thought you people would know what to do with him." That didn't sound right, so I added, "How to help him."

Just then a door at the back of the office opened and a gentleman stepped out. He wore a soft gray flannel suit, and, although it was the middle of August, a snug vest. A patterned blue tie was knotted in a perfect double Windsor, and a triangle of a folded handkerchief decorated his vest pocket. His lapel pin was a gold-framed American flag. I'd seen the pictures; it was Lawrence Lafonte. He had a gentle face with bushy gray eyebrows and a wide nose that was humbled by a thick mustache. He looked like your kind Uncle Larry, the uncle who didn't molest you when you were seven.

"Is Samson ready with the car?" he asked Sybil.

"Yes, Mr. Lafonte," she replied politely. "Are you off to the city?"

"Yes. Have to see our taxman. And what is this?" he said gently, looking at the cat, or maybe at Sybil's cleavage.

"This gentleman here has a homeless cat. He'd like us to help."

"Well, that's not exactly our business," Mr. Lafonte said. "But why not take him to Marcus. I think he could use something to do." As Lafonte went back into his office, he called back, "And tell her the car's ready."

"Yes sir," Sybil answered. "Come with me. Marcus is the new head of accounting, he's just down the hall." She handed Cat-Meow back to me.

I followed Sybil down the hall. I hadn't realized how tall she was. She glided ahead of me, her dress floating about her. I followed obediently. I scratched Cat-Meow behind the ears. He purred happily. I could see 'into the offices on both sides of the hallway and was getting the impression that only pretty young women wanted to save kittens. This place was loaded with potential affair-bait. Marcus was the first guy I saw; he worked in an office with two women. ACCOUNTING was lettered on the door. One of his office mates was the infamous

Vera Booby; the other was a solid girl with wide shoulders and short blond hair. I remembered the name Thalia Davidson. All three were concentrating on their computer screens, but Marcus had propped his balding head up on one hand so he could doze while appearing to study a spreadsheet. He wasn't the prettiest guy I'd ever seen. His head was mostly free of any hair, except for a few tufts around the edge and the hair that stuck out of his ears. He was wearing a shiny blue suit made in China from chemical waste. The snoring didn't lend credibility to his assumed studiousness. Sybil motioned for me to go in, then called to the back of the office, "Vera. Lover boy says the car is ready."

Vera looked up, laughed, and said, "Tell him I'll be there in a minute."

Vera? Vera's riding with Lafonte to the station? I have to follow this. Marcus hadn't moved, so I placed Cat-Meow quietly on his desk. When I left, he was gently nuzzling Marcus's arm, trying to wake him from his slumber. I hurried down the hall, waved to Sybil on the way out. Before she could respond, I was out the door. I walked by Samson waiting by the limo and crossed the street. Half-way up the hill into the Park, I figured I was out of his view, so I took off at a dead run. Number Six watched curiously as I raced by. I ran through the Park and down the driveway beside LeRoy's to my car in the back. By the time I'd driven out of the lot and around the Park, I could see the limo pull away from the curb. Out of the corner of my eye I saw Number Six get up from his bench and begin to shuffle away. That means Vera was in the limo with Lafonte, headed for the train station.

It took four blocks to find an opening to get around the limousine. Passing cars in the middle of town on Main Street is not usually a good idea, and it prompted a chorus of angry horn blasts. I ran the next red light and left the limo standing stationary at the intersection. I arrived at South Station before Lafonte and his date, or I should say, "Lover Boy" and Vera Booby.

7

The commuters, those who lived in town but chose to work in the city, or those who worked in the city and chose to live in our town, took the train every day from South Station. A few drove; they were the commuters who wanted to spend a few extra hours a day away from their families. The south-bound morning trains to the city were crowded; the south-bound evening trains full of empty seats. Lafonte would take one of these, the 6:10 to the city. I skidded to a stop in a space in the parking lot, jumped out, and ran for the station. Running for trains was normal—no one stared. I was in the waiting room leaning against a wall by the door when Lafonte's limo turned the corner. It pulled up in front of the station exactly as the train whistle sounded its approach. Mr. Lafonte emerged, turned, and held the door. Two bare legs appeared, followed by a micro mini, two large breasts, and a blaze of red hair. Looks like Vera Booby to me. They came into the waiting room, a large sterile space, terrazzo floors and bare walls. The old wooden benches along the sides were left over from the time before the station was modernized and steril-ized. The few passengers who had been waiting were fold-ing their newspapers and moving toward the arriving train. Mr. Lafonte, red-faced and fuming, walked straight through

to the platform. Vera headed for the ladies room. I walked out
to the platform as the train rolled into the station. A handful
of passengers left the train; the few waiting on the platform
climbed aboard. Mr. Lafonte followed. Vera was not with
him. I waited but Vera didn't appear. The train jerked, pulled
ahead, picked up speed, and rolled away, shrinking down the
tracks, headed for the big city. I was sorry not to be aboard.
New York; I hadn't been there for a while and I was looking
forward to the chance to live out a few old memories.

Running to the bathroom and missing the train is not a
good way to consummate a clandestine tryst. I checked out
front; I thought the limo was gone, but then I spotted it at
the end of the parking lot. I'll try the bar. The Coliseum
Bar leaned against the north wall of the station. It used to be
called Pete's, but someone put fiberglass columns on either
side of the door and renamed it the Coliseum Bar. One could
enter directly from the station waiting room through a side
door. I followed a middle-aged couple, and we had to squeeze
by a wide-shouldered guy standing beside the door. The black
shined shoes and the baseball cap seemed to say "undercover
cop." We were followed by a young man wearing a red plaid
shirt, khakis, hiking boots, with a backpack slung over one
shoulder. The guy was a walking advertisement for L.L. Bean.
Vera was perched on a stool in front of the bar. An all-too-in-
terested bartender set a dark draft beer before her. I picked up
an abandoned copy of *The Alternate View*, found a table by the
window, motioned to the waiter, and ordered myself a draft.
Just wanted to fit in.

L.L. Bean guy looked around the room, then walked over
and took a stool next to Vera. She did stand out, and I guess he
decided there was nothing to lose by trying. The relationship
didn't last long. He only said a few words before he gulped
down the rest of his soda and left the bar.

Vera wasn't at ease. She shifted on her stool and looked around, as though she was waiting for someone. Her eyes fell on me. I wondered if she recognized me from the office. I tipped my glass toward her as a silent toast and went back to concentrating on the paper. One story caught my eye. Something about how many kittens are abandoned in countries around the world, abandoned to wander hopelessly and alone, mewing pathetically in the back alleys of a dying slum. The story was illustrated with a picture of a very sad kitten. I wondered how much KittyLuv had slipped the reporter to get this story into the paper. In the corner of my eye I saw Vera slide off her stool and start in my direction. I turned the page and studiously concentrated on the paper.

"Mind if I join you?" Vera was standing over me.

"Please be my guest." I looked up and motioned to an empty chair.

"Do I know you from somewhere?" she asked.

"Sounds like a pick-up line to me."

Vera looked at the paper. "You're reading the personals?" She said pointing toward the open page. "You're alone in a bar. You must be looking for company?"

"Just checking for old friends."

"Well," Vera looked me in the eye. "I did see you at the office with that cat—makes me feel that I can trust you. I have a proposition for you."

"I accept." I smiled.

"No. Not what you think. It's just that I, I mean, I was wondering if you could walk me home."

I sat up a bit straighter. "Afraid of the dark?"

"Well, yes. Sort of. I'd feel better if there was someone with me."

"Where's home?"

"Just a few blocks from here. You can leave that." She pointed to the half-finished beer. "I'll fix you a real drink if we get there."

It sounded like an offer I couldn't refuse, even if the "if we get there" was a bit unnerving. I stood, dropped a ten on the table, and followed the lovely motion of Vera's hips out the door.

The fresh outdoor air was a welcome contrast with the smoky bar. The sun had set, and a clouded sky had hastened the onset of the dark of the evening. Vera started to walk along Lincoln Avenue, by the parking lot. "I really should introduce myself. My name's Vera."

"I'm Blue," I answered. "I mean I'm called Blue. Glad to meet you."

"It's down that road over there." Vera pointed to an intersection ahead. "I'm about a quarter of a mile down there." She took my arm, letting her breast nudge me in the direction of the road ahead.

I could barely read the sign on the corner, Corncob Road, an old tarred road that wound past a few factories that bordered the rail yards. I knew the road; it curved by the rail yard for about a half-mile to a dead end, a favorite parking spot for teenagers in love. The factories along the side were the dark shapes I could see from my fire escape, old and abandoned. The trains had cut back freight service years ago, and the factories died or moved out of town, where they relied on trucks and highways to carry their freight.

Unused freight cars stood idly about the rail yard. I remember standing by the tracks and watching the boxcars slowly rolling by. I once counted a hundred cars pulled by two tandem steam engines. I was jealous of the history carried in the names on the boxcars: the Erie Lackawanna, Chesapeake and Ohio, Southern Pacific. Perhaps that is why I live in the

Arms, on the hill overlooking the tracks. I could watch the trains come and go, leaving for another world and then returning with stories to tell. Now, from my window I watch a locomotive push a few coal cars around, but essentially the freight service is dead, the tracks unused and rusting away. The shiny new electric passenger trains that clicked in and out of South Station live elsewhere.

8

We turned the corner and started down Corncob Road. The asphalt was broken into pieces, rain had left deep ruts, and the last street light was on the corner we'd left behind. The silhouettes of abandoned factories loomed ahead. I couldn't see anything that resembled a house, and I was skeptical that anyone actually lived on Corncob Road.

Vera anticipated my question. "I know. It doesn't look like anyone could live here. But when it's late, sometimes I don't want to go all the way to the city so I stay in an old factory."

"Is that the Bishop Pipe Factory?" I remembered the name.

"Yes. My father owned it. He was an old-time factory guy. Worked his way up until he eventually owned the place, but it's deserted now. We're almost there—it's just around the bend."

We walked on, without talking. I began thinking of the scene I'd somehow let myself be caught in. Perhaps this was an elaborate ruse. I would walk along the deserted road. A car would pass by slowly, and stop a few yards ahead. The doors would open and bright lights shine in my eyes. The back seat of a long Cadillac beckoned. It was pitch black inside. "Get in!" a deep voice ordered. I got in. A woman snuggled in beside me. She didn't appear to wearing much. We drove until we reached an abandoned warehouse. The man's voice gave the orders. "This is the place, get him out." I smelled perfume and heard a woman's speak. "He looks okay. Are the girls ready?" I was pushed toward the door of the warehouse. Bright spotlights blinded me. "Did you check the size of his dick?" she asked. Deep voice answered, "I'm told it's good— should look okay on film. Get the cameras ready. Quiet on the set. Action . . ." I was wondering what they'd call the film when Vera interrupted my starring role.

"Home is where the sewer pipes are. We're here." She pointed to a large open gate. We stood before an imposing hulk, a factory built of glacial stones. Pipes were piled in front, some stacked neatly, most just thrown around. Rusted, piled, scattered, broken pipes. Massive sewer pipes three feet in diameter, water lines twenty feet long, smaller one-inch gas lines and electrical conduit. The only working machine in the lot was a compact, two-door, white Ford Focus parked in front. We stood inside the gate gazing at the impressive pipe sculptures and the huge shadow of the stone structure over-looking them.

"Wow!" was all I could come up with. "Why did it close?"

"Technology changed, demand collapsed. Dad went broke, and so did his heart. I think it killed him."

"It's yours now?" I asked.

"Yes. I have a loft on the second floor. Come on." We followed a path through the pipes to a side door. Vera took a ring of keys from her bag and opened the padlock. She slid the bolt aside and pushed the door. It opened reluctantly with a deep groan. We were facing a large cavernous space. She switched on a single overhead bulb. The abandoned factory space stretched out before us. The dim light didn't reach the back walls. A graveyard of iron dinosaurs loomed before us in a ghostly glow. A series of machines formed a line along the center of the space, disappearing into the darkness at the far end. Pipes lay on the assembly line that stretched away from us, as if the operation were shut down with no notice given. Wide leather belts criss-crossed the ceiling and ran over pulleys to descend vertically to bring power to the devices below. A soot-covered furnace rose to the ceiling. It used to blaze with a fearsome heat and exhume molten metal, but today it stood cold and still. A giant press stood to one side, its threatening jaws permanently rusted open. Parallel with the central row of machines was a thirty-foot long lathe that cradled a pipe nearly a foot in diameter. Benches against the wall were littered with bits of metal, hammers, files, and wrenches. The scraps of metal that were scattered about the floor were covered with a thick coal dust. A single work glove lay, palm up, at my feet. The silent motionless machines left over from an industrial age were patiently waiting. Waiting to create another pipe.

"Beautiful, aren't they." Vera was admiring the classic machines. "This will be a museum. These guys are unique." She referred to the huge creatures as though they were her buddies. "They're irreplaceable. The Bishop Machine Museum. My Dad would like that. Someday," she said dreamily. A narrow set of wooden stairs rose along the side wall. The machines watched us as we started up. One step complained so loudly I thought it was about to crack and send us back into the arms of the nasty-looking pipe crusher below us. At a small landing twenty-five feet up, Vera found another key on the ring and we entered her apartment. I was faced with total blackness until Vera reached around behind the door to flip the master switch in the fuse box. The place came alive. A huge room with ceilings that must be at least twenty feet high. Four lamps hung by chains from the ceiling to shaded bulbs. Bookshelves covered the walls from floor to ceiling on two sides. They were packed, row after row of books, with more stuffed in on their sides. The floor was concrete, but Vera had covered it with classic oval rag rugs. A long flat table in the middle surrounded by a few wooden chairs gave the place the flavor of a hidden library. An open curtain at the far end revealed a single bed and a standing closet. A small kitchen was built against one wall, looking as if it didn't really belong there. I sat on the one piece of comfortable furniture, a large overstuffed couch in front of the bookshelves.

Vera broke the silence. "I don't stay here all the time. I have an apartment in the city, but this is awfully convenient if I'm tired, or just want to be alone. Can I get you a drink? What would you like?"

"Do you serve martinis here?"

"No. But I do have scotch."

"Sounds good me, with a couple of ice cubes to stretch it a bit."

Vera walked over to the kitchen. I looked over the shelves behind the couch. An encyclopedia of industries, manuals from machine shops, a book of photographs of old industrial sites, the autobiography of Henry Ford. Vera brought two glasses, each filled to the brim with a well-aged Jameson, and sat down next to me on the sofa.

"To Vera," I smiled and raised my glass, simultaneously putting my hand on her soft knee.

"Boo, I have a confession to make."

"It's Blue."

Vera didn't hear me. "I actually didn't bring you here to make love."

"Let me guess. You're a virgin."

"No. Actually I'd love to make love to you. But that's not really why I picked you up and asked you to come home with me."

"You thought you were being followed."

Vera nodded. "How did you know that?"

A sharp cracking sound! The broken stair. Vera froze. "Oh my God!" She whispered.

I didn't ask, just went to the door and listened. All was quiet. "Tell me something Vera. Quick! Who's out there? What's he want?"

"It's the letter. He wants the letter." She was interrupted by a loud banging on the door.

"Letter?" I whispered. "What letter?"

"I have to take it, Boo. I'll go out the back. Please, just keep him busy for a second. And," Vera looked at me, "don't tell anyone!" She pulled open the top drawer of the bureau, pulled too hard and too fast, and it fell to the floor. At that moment with a sharp blast, splinters of wood flew across the room. The lock on the door was blown half off. Vera ran toward the back of the loft and grabbed the emergency handle of a fire escape door. A second bullet blew through the lock. The door flew off its hinges and crashed to the floor. I was pushed behind the door—against the wall, the fuse box jabbing me in the back. I grabbed blindly, caught hold of the master switch, and yanked it down. As a figure burst into the room the loft disappeared into a solid black mystery. I heard him slam into the table and crash to the ground.

A faint light came through from the open fire escape door. I could hear Vera's footsteps as she ran down the metal fire stairs. I didn't move. The shadowy form stumbled into a chair and spewed out a series of "Shits" and "Fucks." I saw his form outlined in the faint light of the fire doorway, then vanish outside. I didn't have a plan, but it seemed like trying to keep Vera from getting shot would be the gentlemanly thing to do. Anything I could do to distract would help. I pushed the power switch back up and the loft lit up in a blaze. I could hear him thumping down the fire escape after Vera. I was about to take the reverse route down the front stairs, when I saw an envelope among the contents of the drawer that were scattered on the floor. I quickly scooped it up and ran down the stairs we came in by to the pipe-filled yard in time to see the taillights of Vera's Ford disappear around the bend. I hid behind a tall pile of sewer mains and peered around the edge.

The night was strangely quiet. The intruder was standing with his back to me waving his gun at the road. He was wearing a sweatshirt with the hood pulled over his head. I took the envelope out of my pocket, slipped it into a small pipe in the pile. If I lost this fight, at least he wasn't getting the fucking letter. I groped around the junk on the ground and found a three-foot piece of steel water pipe, which unfortunately scraped against its neighbor as I pulled it out. He spun around and turned on a flashlight, which shined directly in my eyes. I couldn't see much, so I swung the pipe. I think I hit his arm, as the flashlight flew into the pile of pipes. He grabbed for the light, still shining from the ground.

This guy is nasty, about to get his light back, and has a gun. This is not a fight I should pick. I took off at a dead run around the back of the factory. I am fast, it was pitch dark, and I was fifty yards into the cornfield before he dug the flashlight out of the pile of pipes. He didn't take up the chase, and I watched from the distance as his silhouette disappeared around the factory wall. I didn't get a good look at him. All I knew was that he was tall, thin, and nasty, carried a gun, and had a sore arm. I circled around behind the factory, feeling my way through the woods as quietly as I could, until I was in sight of the station. I waited—no use rushing this.

A half hour later I crossed the Avenue to the lot and the comfort of my Beamer, and the comfort of the Glock that was under the front seat. Vera didn't want me to say anything.

"Don't tell anybody," she had pleaded. Maybe she is hiding something; maybe she wants to protect someone. Her call—I'll let her report this if she wants. I'm just an observer. I watch, I listen, and there will be time to think about tonight, tomorrow.

9

I lay awake much of the night trying to make sense of my evening with Vera. An affair, a letter, a scary nutcase with a gun, all in a dead factory watched over by silent machines. I finally fell asleep dreaming of a land of pipes, pipes that moved, that stood on end, and danced and spoke in hollowed voices. I found myself inside a huge sewer pipe. An envelope floated before me, just out of reach. I chased it through an endless tunnel. The sides shrank around me as I ran, then crawled, then slid on my stomach through a pipe no larger around than my chest. I sat upright, with a start, pushing the dream away. I wondered if I would be able to find that letter, which, foolishly, I'd stuffed in some pipe somewhere in the midst of vast pipe graveyard.

The sun had crept over the horizon when Doctor Dollar's receptionist, June of the shining blond hair, called. She said he could meet me as soon as he took care of his paying clients for the day. I ignored the hint, and said I would be by after lunch. I was sure that one of these days I'd be able to send a big job in his direction. I doubt the Doctor expected that, but he was too nice to tell me to add up my own numbers. When I arrived at his office, the waiting room was empty and the Doctor was alone in his office.

"Good day, Doctor."

Henry Cadman rose from behind his desk and put out his hand. "Sorry I missed you the other day. Blue, how have you been?"

"Fine, Doctor, and you're looking good." He'd lost some of his extra pounds and the old tan suit that had struggled to contain him for the past year or so was proudly showing a waistline.

"Yes. I know. Started exercising—can you imagine such a thing?"

"No. Afraid I can't. But you're a good advertisement for it."

Tired of the small talk, the Doctor sat back down and looked at the notes before him. "So when did this interest in kittens come over you?"

"A job's a job. Sometimes work requires real compromises. Did you come up with anything?"

"Benny took a quick look through their site and browsed around the Internet for a bit. KittyLuv's a well-funded charity. I didn't know homeless kittens would bring in that kind of money. Blue, you're definitely in the wrong business."

"So, does Mr. Lafonte haul in some eight figure salary?"

"Actually, his salary is modest, well below what would upset the donors, at least on the surface. Aside from the salary, he gets a car and driver and some kind of cost-of-living subsidy."

"Health care, retirement, et cetera," I added.

"Of course. Also his appearance is important, so he can deduct everything from his suits to the cost of trimming his mustache."

"I've been by the house—or rather the mansion, and I've seen his wife's diamonds. He'd have to fake a lot of mustache work to pay for those."

The Doctor rubbed his chin, looking the part of a thought-ful economist. "Benny dug around there a bit; that certainly is an expensive operation. I doubt Lafonte's salary would cover it, but he may have a nest egg we didn't catch."

"What about Louella Lafonte? Any family money?"

"No money at all in her background. Her mother was a teacher in a small town in Hungary. Her father disappeared early on. Her mother brought her to the States when she was about ten. She didn't go to college and spent much of her life at low-level jobs, waitressing and such. Then she met Law-rence Lafonte and things changed."

"Sounds like she's searching for elegance."

"One other thing I ran across. You know that staff photo-graph on the KittyLuv website?"

"Yes. A bevy of young pretty gals."

"But it's the guy who caught my eye."

"Doctor. You never told me."

Doctor Dollar ignored me. "The bald guy, with the funny tufts of hair."

"And some growing out of his ears?" I'd met the guy. "Mar-cus Doolittle. He works in accounting."

"I've seen him before," the Doctor explained. "A couple of years ago I was called to testify at a fraud case in the city. The DA was suing a guy named Hamilton. I was testifying for one of my clients who lost a bunch in Hamilton's Ponzi scheme. It wasn't a big-time operation, but big enough to catch the eye of the authorities. Hamilton was an eager beaver hedge fund manager who was trying to get rich quick. He wasn't very good at it; the whole scheme fell apart before it even took off.

"Where's Doolittle in this?"

"Doolittle was part of Hamilton's staff. He was a low-lev-el accountant and wasn't charged with anything, but I was struck at the trial by how quickly Doolittle turned against his boss. He was a fountain of damning information. Hamilton got sent away for a couple of years, and Doolittle walked away. The operation came across as downright seedy, and, if I say so myself, not very professional."

"You could have done it a lot better?"

The Doctor frowned. "Damn right I could, but . . ."

"But you're just too downright honest."

The Doctor's frown turned to a smile. "Maybe you could give me a few pointers, when you get a chance."

"Be glad to, Doc, but right now I have to pick up some mail. I'm expecting an important letter."

10

As I turned onto Corncob Road, a titanic truck thundered out, forcing me off the tarred road. It was loaded with pipes. What the hell—those rusted pipes aren't worth anything, even as scrap. I turned back onto the road and started toward Vera's factory home. The scene before me brought me to a halt in front of the broken gate. I was facing a bustling construction site, or, more accurately, a deconstruction site. A huge grunting, creaking back-loader was forcing its nose under a mass of pipes, loading them onto another giant dump truck. Workers were climbing over the piles, rolling pipes into position for loading. I jumped out but was confronted by a large menacing character with a bulge under his overcoat that barely concealed a weapon that could stop a tank. His head was covered with a wire brush that was masquerading as a haircut. I'd seen this guy somewhere before.

"Whoa! Off limits, guv!" He shouted. "Men working."

"You can't do that!" I protested.

"Who the fuck says so?"

"I know the owner," I shouted back over the din of the machines. "I want to talk to her."

"No owner, man. She moved out yesterday. The building's coming down."

I was jolted by a crash, and two stones on the far corner of the factory itself came tumbling down. A large bulldozer showed its teeth around the edge of the building and prepared to take another bite. Damn! The building, the pipes, and where did I put that envelope? The pipes along the path to the front door were still untouched, and that's where I'd shoved it into a pipe.

"You have a demolition permit?" I challenged.

"None of your business!" the brute yelled back. "Just get your ass off the property!"

I needed help, and I knew where to get it; I hope Captain JJ Cakes is in today. I hurried back to my car, backed it across the road, and flipped open my cell. The Captain's secretary answered and put me through. The guard looked at me suspiciously as I talked on the phone with JJ. Nothing to do now but hope JJ can get here before the letter gets carted away. I sat in the car, rolled down the window, and waited. I watched the guard. He stood in the middle of the road forming a barrier between me and the demolition. An image came to mind—the large guy standing by the door at the Coliseum Bar the night I met Vera, who I thought was an undercover cop. He isn't the same guy who chased Vera—this guy is as wide as a bulldozer blade. I never saw the face of the thug who shot his way through the factory, but he was tall and thin.

Twenty minutes later another truckful of pipes rolled off the lot, and the backhoe rolled closer to the path. I was considering making a run for the envelope, but I wasn't really sure which pipe it was hiding in. I didn't have to. A police car rolled to a stop in front of the gate. I watched JJ calmly climb out and walk up to the wide-shouldered bodyguard. The guard was clearly ready to explode when JJ drew a citation book from his coat, opened it up, and started to write. The guard waved toward the workers, and a guy in a hard hat—I figured he was the foreman—climbed up on some pipes and yelled to the guard, "Hey, Knockout. What's the problem here?" Knockout—not a bad name for wire head. Pretty soon the foreman had joined the discussion and was waving his hands, spitting on the ground, and about to burst a blood vessel. Then, beaten, he turned toward the band of workers who were standing motionless, watching the drama, and waved them off. The machines were shut down, and the scene became quiet and still. I'd guessed right, they didn't have demolition permit. As Vera "moved out" as they called it, only a day ago, this was a last-minute decision. They didn't have time to get a permit, even from our eminently bribable Department of Buildings.

JJ got back into the squad car, never giving a glance in my direction, threw it into reverse, and turned around. The foreman was calling after him, "Damn it! We'll be back tomorrow with your damn permit." JJ drove away. The guard and the foreman started across the road toward me. Good time to leave. Actually ten minutes ago would have been a good time to leave. The foreman was at my window, and he was plenty pissed.

"I don't know what you're after," he yelled at me. "You shouldn't mess with DR. They're bigger than your whole God-damn town!"

I said, "Sorry, but I kinda like the gal who lives here."

"You rotten son-of-a-bitch," the foreman raged. He grabbed his hardhat and was about to try to put it through my front window when Knockout took his arm.

"Don't do that, Jack. You'll just get in trouble." He turned toward me with a tight grin. "There are better ways to deal with punks like this. Trust me."

I trusted him and thought it was a good time to leave. I pressed on the gas, and watched the men shrinking in my rear view mirror, standing in the middle of Corncob Road discussing the various ways they were going to castrate me. It's Thursday. They won't be able to get a permit and start again before Monday at the earliest. The pipes by the path haven't been moved yet—I'll wait until things quiet down and come by over the weekend to pick up my mail.

11

Captain JJ Cakes had left a message on my cell. "Okay, Blue. What the hell was that all about? Come by the office. I'm in tomorrow afternoon."

Before I met JJ, I had time to stop by the Buildings Department. Charles was there in the mornings, which would make my job a lot easier. I parked behind LeRoy's and walked up the driveway to the Park. The courthouse looked over the Park. It was built early in the century when every American town was modeling its government buildings on the style of the Parthenon—wide steps in front, imposing ionic columns framing the entrance. Inside, a grand lobby rose four floors above a patterned marble floor. Balconies circled each level overhead, and a domed ceiling was waiting for Michelangelo to come and decorate. The grandiose entrance was misleading, however, as the Buildings Department was one of a mishmash of offices stuffed into an unimpressive money-saving addition tacked on the back of the building. Signs led me out the back of the lobby and down a drab hallway of office doors, until I found one labeled Department of Buildings. A dull-eyed receptionist looked up and was about to give me a number, when I caught Charles's eye through the open door of his office. He got up from his desk and came out to welcome me.

"Greetings, Blue. How have you been?"

"Fine, Charley, fine. You look good. How's the home front?"

"We're all good, and I'm a grandfather again. Who'd have thought?"

"Congratulations. Nicely done."

"Like I had anything to do with it. So what can I do for you?" Charles asked with his usual cheer.

We sat down in his office, and I got right to the point. "You know the old Bishop Pipe Factory? It's one of the old, closed-down factories near South Station."

"Yep. A couple of guys were in here this morning about that."

"Really? That was fast."

Charles looked at the sign-in ledger. "A Mr. Sidney Jones. You just missed him."

"The other guy, did he give a name?"

"No, but I'd recognize him anywhere. Not that many people have more hair growing out of their ears than on the top of their head."

I laughed. "Asking for a permit, I figure."

"How'd you know that?" Charles asked.

"I interrupted a work crew yesterday. They weren't very happy about it."

"You mean they'd already started. Not legal!" Charles was annoyed. "We haven't seen any plans, we didn't give them an okay."

"Did you give the guy Jones a permit this morning?"

"Hell no! They don't exactly own the place."

"Who is the they?"

"DR, Diamond Realty. They're a big real estate firm based in New York. Jones said they had an option to buy the land.

I had to tell him that wasn't enough, that he needed proof of ownership."

"This Jones guy. If he's works for a real estate company, he has to know he can't get a permit without proof of ownership."

"I think he had other ideas," Charley said with a tight grin. "When he tried to find his glasses, he pulled his wallet out and laid it between us. It was stuffed with bills. Diamond Realty is used to getting what they want."

"Ah, business as usual. So, Charley, how many did you take?"

Charles laughed a humorless laugh. "Blue, I'm six months away from retirement. Wouldn't want to risk it all at this stage. Jones stomped out in a bit of a huff. Said he'd be back. Got my curiosity up, so I went downstairs and looked through the files. I remembered that Mr. Bishop came here with some questions about his deed. He had some financial problems and needed a loan to stay afloat. He was offering an option to buy the place as collateral. It would take effect in ten years if he didn't repay the loan. As far as I know, the option was never taken. That was about twenty years ago. Mr. Bishop died and left the factory and the land to his daughter. The deed is in her name, Vera Bishop, but as long as the option remains in effect she has nothing to say about selling it."

"You wouldn't know the price, I suppose?"

"Yes, and given today's prices it would be a steal."

"Thanks, Charley. Very interesting. Don't know what I'd do without you. So any time you could use a little detective work, just let me know."

Charles laughed again, this time with more humor. "Well, let's see. You could check up on my neighbor—he's been looking a bit suspicious lately. Or there's my brother-in-law who owes me a hundred bucks. You might take a peek at him."

"Be glad to." I patted Charley on the shoulder and turned to leave.

"One more thing, Blue. Diamond Realty doesn't hold the option. You might be interested in the name on the agreement." Charles hesitated for effect. "The one who holds the right to buy the place? It's the KittyLuv guy, you know. Lawrence Lafonte."

12

The police headquarters was at the top of the Park next to the courthouse. I knew it well. They'd paid me for undercover assignments over the years, usually for work that the police department didn't want to be caught doing. The young fresh-faced recruit behind the front desk, Patrolman Thomas, was eager to check my ID, get me to sign in, and assure him that I had an appointment. Fortunately, Inspector Corbutt looked up from his desk. "Hey, Blue, how's things?"

"Not bad, Muscles, not bad. And you're looking good." Corbutt spent his free hours at the local gym, and the result was that he had to have specially tailored uniforms made that wouldn't burst apart when he sneezed.

He turned toward the recruit. "Tom, he's harmless. JJ knows him, he can go on up."

The recruit looked disappointed, but closed the registration book and waved me by. "Captain Cakes has moved. He's still on the fourth floor but at the end of the hall." I nodded respectfully—the kid needed something to make his day—and took the elevator to the fourth floor. Four A was at the far end of the hallway. Captain Cakes was painted on the opaque glass panel in strong Police Department New Roman script. I pushed open the door to the outer office. I almost expected to see the lovely Kathy at the desk, but she had received a bunch of promotions and was now the new Police Chief MacGregor. I always thought that was a bit tough on JJ, but he never complained. His secretary, the intimidating Miss Cumberland, reluctantly put down her telephone.

"Hi, Sweetie." I winked at her.

She tipped her head back to look down at me through her bifocals. "Excuse me. Do you have an appointment?" Miss Cumberland always made me feel as though I was about to receive a spanking.

"JJ asked me to drop by."

"Please sit down, Mr. Heron. He's quite busy, but I'll tell him you're here." The prim and proper Miss C pressed the intercom button. "Mr. Heron to see you, sir."

The crackle of static that responded from the speaker must have been positive, for Miss C said, "Captain Cakes will see you now, Mr. Heron. You may go in." She pointed toward the door to the inner office.

JJ's new office was a pleasant surprise, sitting at the corner of the building with windows on two sides, the larger one facing over the Park. The most amazing part of the scene was JJ's desk. Gone were the piles of files, folders, and reports. JJ sat behind a clean, polished wooden desk sporting only the intercom, a phone, and a picture of his family. He looked up at me and got right to the point.

"So, Blue, what was all that about yesterday?"

"JJ, thanks for helping out. I was in a bind and running out of options."

"Options for what? Tell me something."

"They were hauling the pipes away. I had to stop them somehow."

"Yes, go on." JJ sat back in his chair and folded his arms across his round stomach, resigned to getting a lame-assed explanation.

"I put something in the pipes that I had to get. The guard wasn't about to let me on the site. I figured you could shut down the operation, and you were great."

"And just what did you hide that was so God-damned important?" JJ was trying to stay calm.

"I don't know."

"You don't know?"

"Nope, afraid not, until I get it."

JJ sighed and scratched his balding head. "Let's see. I pulled police rank to shut down an operation so you could get, hmmm, something."

"Yes. Might be important."

"Something, hidden somewhere, that might be important?"

"Look, JJ. Give me a day. I'll go back tonight, after nightfall when the place has quieted down, and I'll tell you what I find."

"Sounds like a lovely idea, Blue. The police department has made it possible for you to sneak into someone's place after dark to find something that maybe is worth finding and then take it."

"Right!" I smiled reassuringly.

"Fine." JJ's voice was rising. "What have I got to lose? Using police power to help a private citizen steal something. That should look good on my record. You've always told me I should spend more time with my family. Well, maybe I'm looking at a chance for early retirement." JJ was clearly agitated. "Blue! Get the hell out of here, and you'd better come back with a good explanation. Oh, and if you get shot at for trespassing, don't call the police."

"Thanks, JJ. Knew I could count on you. Give my best to the wife and kids."

On the way out of the office, I gave Miss C another wink. "How about a date Saturday night? Just a drink, and who knows." I suspected that the tight Miss C didn't take her gray suit skirt off when she retired for the night. She ignored me and continued talking with her friend on the telephone. I let myself out.

13

I thanked Patrolman Thomas at the front desk and was at the door when I heard a familiar voice call my name. "Blue. Just a second."

"Kathy. What's up?" I smiled, but Kathy was all business. No flirting today.

"A call just came in. Hard to figure out, 911 said the caller was hysterical. Something's gone wrong over at the rail yards. Thomas, call Captain Cakes. Tell him he's needed down here ASAP."

"What's it got to do with me?"

"JJ told me that you were at the rail yards last night."

It's hard to scare me, but I remembered Vera running off, and I remembered the madman who was after her with a gun. "Do you know what happened? Anybody hurt?" I asked as calmly as I could.

"More than that, I'm afraid. Apparently the 911 call was a bunch of screams. The caller kept yelling, 'It's awful! It's awful!'"

Kathy saw JJ coming down the hall and said, or rather ordered, "Okay. Let's go!" The police cars pulled up before we were down the front steps, Kathy's black-and-white Chief of Police car was first, followed by a squad car. Kathy jumped in hers and was on her way, with lights flashing and the siren wailing, before JJ and I could even get seated. Corbutt was driving, JJ sat up front, and I was in back. Normally I'd get a charge out of tearing through town with sirens blasting, but I was thinking of Vera. Cars pulled over to the side as we turned off Main Street and onto Lincoln Avenue. Corbutt was following closely behind the Chief. We passed Corncob Road, the station itself, turned onto a road that led into the yards, and drove on between the tracks.

A group of curious spectators was standing next to a Union Pacific boxcar, the last of a row of about twenty stretching off into the distance. Kathy ordered the growing crowd to move back, not to touch anything, and calm down. Someone had thrown a blanket over the body next to the tracks. I restrained myself, and waited, watching Kathy and JJ secure the site and then move to the shape on the ground. Kathy knelt and slowly pulled the blanket back. Identification was not easy—there was no head! A couple of the bystanders screamed, and one guy collapsed in a faint. I leaned forward to look as Kathy uncovered the body. There was blood everywhere, on the ground, soaked into the gravel, and soaking the red-and-black flannel shirt. It's hard to admit to a feeling of relief when looking at a badly mutilated body, but it wasn't Vera.

Someone called out the obvious question, "Where's his head?"

One of the bystanders waved his arm, and pointed to the boxcar. He was right. A bloody head lay beneath the car, between the tracks. I followed Kathy to the rails, to the gruesome sight. What was left of a face was unrecognizable.

JJ, in his usual unruffled style, pointed and explained. "The body must have been on the tracks, the head on the rails. Train must have run over his neck when it was pushed backwards along the tracks and . . ." He made a motion across his neck.

Kathy called to Corbutt. "Inspector, get the forensic team, and call the mortuary." JJ walked over to the bystanders and began taking down names and contact information. Kathy's driver handed her a pair of rubber gloves, and she knelt down to search the body. I admired the way Chief MacGregor waded into a case. No passing the tough jobs off—she would give clear orders and then work side by side along with her staff. She retrieved some dollars, some change, a pen, and placed them in plastic evidence bags. "No wallet," she said to no one in particular. I looked for the backpack and found it in a pool of water some yards away, surrounded by garbage. It was shredded and lying open. I didn't touch it—police procedure—but studied it closely. Corbutt came over and marked the spot with yellow tape. He pulled on his gloves and carefully gathered up the pack. I was about to walk back when something glistened in the mud. I poked at it, a few small plastic bags clumped together. I carefully pulled the top one off. It came away from the one beneath leaving a clean surface, which meant it wasn't garbage as I had thought. I pointed them out to Corbutt.

The forensic team arrived and cordoned off the site, and sent the bystanders away. I stood with Kathy and JJ by the Chief's car. She asked the first question, "Blue. You were here last night. Right?"

"Not exactly. I was at the pipe factory, over there." We could see the back of the factory on the far side of the tracks.

"Can you tell us anything?" Kathy pressed.

I thought about it before answering. "I've seen him before."

Both Kathy and JJ perked up.

"Three nights ago. I saw him in the station. In the Coliseum Bar. He came down from the north on the six ten. At least I saw a guy in the same flannel shirt and khakis."

"What was he doing?" Kathy asked.

"He got a soda at the bar and then went out. I don't know whether he got in a car or taxi or what."

"I'd ask what you were doing in the bar, but I don't really want to know," Kathy said under her breath.

"I couldn't see any other signs of murder," JJ wondered. "No gunshot wounds, knife wounds. How do you get a guys head under a boxcar if he's alive?"

I stood by the side, watching the teams at work. The follow-up police work was underway—combing the site, taking samples from the bloody soil, samples of the mud on the victim's boots, photographing the body, categorizing any scrapes in the gravel by the tracks. JJ had taken over the supervision of the investigation, which essentially meant he had to keep the teams from getting into each other's way. The reporters had arrived, and Kathy was attempting to ward off the fusillade of questions.

I was not needed. Corbutt drove me back to the center of town, where I could retrieve my Beamer. On the drive back I wondered about Vera, wondered what the poor guy had said to her in the bar, wondered if she knew him, wondered where she was.

. . . .

I picked up my car and started home. I stopped at Ralph's Pizza on the way. Ate a couple of slices, downed a beer, and tried to flirt with the waitress, but my heart just wasn't in it. Can't say hers was either, and she hadn't recently seen someone without a head. By the time I turned onto Machinist's

Drive the sun was setting and the brightest stars were struggling to be seen. A martini, relaxing in a seat on the fire escape, and the infinity of the night sky might calm my nerves, but I found the dark broken by the bright glow of floodlights from the rail yards. I could barely make out the figures, tiny black shapes moving about; insects randomly searching for food. Strobe lights flashed regularly as the police and the reporters each gathered their own kind of information. They'd be there for a while, digging for clues, and preventing anyone from disturbing the site.

During my second martini, the floodlights suddenly dimmed. The sky took over. I leaned back and found Perseus just as a meteor streaked out and fell down toward the horizon. Its flight started at Algol, the second brightest star in the constellation. Algol is the eye of Medusa. Perseus severed the Gorgon's head and has carried it through the sky ever since. A tear had fallen from the eye of Medusa, a tear of sympathy for the railyard kid.

14

The morning headlines could hardly contain themselves. We hadn't had a beheading in quite a while, not since Farmer Mack's harvester jammed, and he stuck his head in to see what was blocking the blade. *The Journal* proclaimed, in four-inch high letters: HORROR AT THE RAIL YARDS! *The Herald* was more direct: MAN LOSES HIS HEAD! The creative *Alternate View* went poetic with: THE TALE OF THE HEADLESS TRAINMAN! The papers had come out early and no one had identified the victim yet, but that didn't keep the columnists from speculation. It was the result of a drug sale. The mob got angry when this guy was robbing the boxcars of their shipment of cocaine. *The Daily Flyer* found an occult specialist who knew that the beheading was a ritual practiced by an underground cult that met regularly in the basement of the Governor's mansion. The press did show some restraint—they resisted the temptation to display a picture of the severed head.

I called JJ's office, and Miss Cumberland told me he was out of the office. She reluctantly allowed that I could see him Monday afternoon. I looked out over the rail yards. The investigation teams had left, and I could see only one police car parked by the tracks. Tonight, after dark when I won't be spotted, I'll go and retrieve that damn letter.

. . . .

A light rain began just as the sun set. By the time I arrived at South Station, it had turned into a steady drizzle. I was hoping I had stuffed the envelope far enough into the pipe to keep it dry. I parked in the station lot, put on a rainproof slicker, and pulled the hood over my head. I checked my pocket for the small flashlight, crossed the road, and started down Corncob Road. The pipe factory lay ahead. The demolition machines lurked over it like dinosaurs guarding their nest—or whatever dinosaurs raised their babies in. There was only one light to break the gloom. It was the dome light inside the silver SUV parked in front, where I could see the buzz cut on the top of a head that was studying a newspaper. Diamond Realty had left Knockout to watch over the place. Bad luck. I left the road and slowly pushed my way through the bushes toward the back of the factory. I didn't dare use my flashlight; I stumbled and scratched my way through some pretty thick and prickly barberry. I worked my way around to the side wall of the factory and then to the door where Vera and I had entered. The path through the pipes was ahead. If I crawled I could stay below the line of pipes and not be seen. Pretty messy, muddy, and wet, but I guess that's what I get paid for. I crawled to the spot where I had stuffed the envelope, but the pipes had been knocked down and scattered on the path. I stuck my finger into each, one after another, with no luck. I had to chance using the light. If KO was concentrating enough on the paper, maybe he wouldn't notice. The light was a small LCD I kept on my key ring, but in the dark the tiny beam looked like a military searchlight. I looked in one pipe, then another. I heard a car door slam.

"Who's there? What are you doing? Come on out!" The voice was approaching. The light showed the end of a crumbled envelope deep in a pipe, but my fingers weren't long enough to retrieve it. I grabbed the pipe, yanked it out of the pile, and took off running like the proverbial bat out of hell. I didn't think KO would shoot at me, but that was just another of my miscalculations. The first shot hit the wall of the stone building next to my head and sprayed sharp pieces of rock across my cheek. I darted and weaved, and took advantage of the dark and my speed. Two more shots were fired, mostly in frustration. A random pipe got in my way and I went sprawling. I was up in a flash and raced limping into the woods, into the pitch-blackness. I dropped to the ground behind the fallen trunk of an old dead tree and lay in the mud. An eerie silence covered the land, broken only by the soft patter of raindrops. I was lying face down, in the dark, in the rain, in the mud, hiding from some maniac who would like to shoot me. Why? What the hell do I care what is in this envelope? It's only important because other people seem to think so. Five hundred a day to do this? Then I thought of Vera, of the fear in her eyes. So there I was, waiting, until I heard the car door slam again. Knockout was talking with someone on his phone—too far away for me to hear. It was the chance I was hoping for, time for me to get up and leave.

I stumbled my way through the trees alongside Corncob Road until I reached the street in front of the station. I was a sodden muddy mess. There was no traffic, so I ran across the street to my car. There was a scream from nearby in the parking lot, and a couple jumped from a car and fled into the station. I guess the image of a large muddy, slimy creature running with a limp carrying a six-foot pipe was too much for them. I didn't wait to explain. I pushed the pipe over the front seat to the back and started up the old BMW. I drove out of the lot before anyone emerged from the station.

It was well after midnight by the time I drove up to the Arms. I parked beside the abandoned van. The rain had let up a bit, but a steady stream of large drops fell from the wet trees. Javier, my building's super, was in his apartment watching late-night TV when I came through the lobby. He looked out his open door and called out cheerfully, "Good night, Blue."

That's why I live in the Arms—a run-down old building full of deadbeats and hideaways and misfits. It was the only place I knew where limping home in the middle of the night coated with mud and carrying a six-foot pipe would not raise an eyebrow.

15

I flattened the crushed envelope on the table. It was small and square—the type used for Christmas cards, thank you notes, or letters of condolence. I recognized the KittyLuv logo on the front. "Larry" was handwritten below the logo.

It had been opened, and I carefully slid a card out and unfolded it. I was greeted by the cute fuzzy face of a calico kitten. Below it, printed in a stylish script: Kitty _____—a blank space left for the name of the cute little fellow—thanks you for giving her a new life. May the Lord be with you.

The signature of Larry Lafonte was printed at the bottom.

I turned the card over. The handwritten message on the back was simple and direct.

Dear Larry Darling,

I miss you—you adorable kitten. I miss your kisses. I want you inside me, like before. When can we meet again? Soon, please.
Love, love, love . . . and kisses.

It was signed: "*Sweetie*."

Sweetie? That's a big help. Maybe Vera's nickname is Sweetie. Maybe there's a kitten named Sweetie. Maybe I was thinking this note was going to answer all my questions. Well, it did answer one——there's definitely a steamy affair underway.

16

The Lafonte mansion sat at the end of a tree-lined cul-de-sac that was more suited to chauffeured limousines than old rusted BMWs. A fine example of the stone architecture of the old wealth, it seemed ill at ease with the self-important McMansions on either side. I was supposed to park around the back, but I stopped directly in front of the marble-tiled porch. Large standing flowerpots framed the doorway. I knocked, then pressed the buzzer. After a long wait with no answer, I peered through the vertical glass pane beside the thick oak door and saw Mrs. Lafonte coming down a grand curved stairway. She opened the door and, obviously surprised to see me, invited me in to a large entrance hall. Louella was not the elegant lady I'd met the other day. She was wearing a loose-fitting dress, slip-on shoes, and no make-up, which led me to imagine a scene in the bedroom at the top of the stairs. She led me into a salon off to the side of the entrance hall. We sat stiffly in two straight-back antique chairs. She didn't offer me anything to drink. I don't think she wanted me to hang around.

Louella got right to the point. "Mr. Heron. Did you find anything?"

"Yes and no." I thought it best not to waste time with sweet talk. "I'm sorry to tell you, but I have some pretty solid evidence that an affair has been going on between your husband and, and somebody."

"Louella perked up. "Yes? What have you found?"

I reached inside my coat, pushed the Glock out of the way, and took out the envelope. I handed it to Lulu. She opened the envelope, unfolded the card, and read silently. A wisp of a smile crossed her face.

"Who's Sweetie?" she asked.

"I'm afraid I don't know. Have no idea at all."

"Where did you find this?"

I hesitated for a moment—this was going to be a bit awkward. "I don't want to say. I don't want to implicate anyone before I have some proof."

"This looks like proof to me!"

I tried to appease her. "It is pretty good proof that an affair is going on. But I don't know where the card was found so it doesn't tell us who the guilty lady is."

Lulu put the card back into the envelope. She reached over her shoulder to the bookshelf, pulled out a book, an old edition of *Alice In Wonderland*, opened it, and slipped the envelope in by the Cheshire Cat. The idea made me smile.

"What's so funny?" Lulu demanded.

When I didn't answer, she asked, "Who found it?"

"I can't say just yet."

She stared at me. I tried to reason with her. "I think that the card is sufficient in and of itself for your divorce, Mrs. Lafonte. But I can keep looking for something more. Chances are I can find out who wrote it."

Lulu looked at me, frowned, then got up and walked to a desk in the corner. She opened a drawer, took out a checkbook, found a pen, and started to write. I looked around the room as I waited. The salon was nicely furnished in the style of the last century, and brightly lit by windows on two sides.

The landscapes hanging on the wall reminded me of those I'd seen in the American wing of the Metropolitan. A fireplace that hadn't been used in a while was at the far end, and a closed door next to the fireplace probably led to a side hall or a room with large windows that scattered the light that shone underneath the doorway, where I could see a shadow that wasn't there a moment ago.

Lulu left her desk and handed me a check. "I think the note is enough. You don't have to find out who she is. I know. It's that Vera Booby bitch, but you're right. That doesn't really matter. If I need anything else I'll call you." She stood, waiting for me to go.

"Nice working for you, Mrs. Lafonte. Just let me know if you need some follow-up."

"Mr. Heron," she called after me.

I turned.

"You kept a copy, didn't you?"

I nodded. She scowled at me, but knew she wasn't going to talk me out of it. "All right. That won't make any difference. Goodbye Mr. Heron."

I let myself out. That was quick. I couldn't complain about the size of the check I was holding in my hand, but I did wonder who had been listening through the door at the side of the salon.

I drove round the circular drive and back onto the through street. Halfway down the block, I pulled over and parked. I walked down a side street that led to the back of the mansion. The gate was open and a gardening crew was working on the grounds. One guy was using a leaf blower to scatter debris toward the neighbor's lawn, and the other gardener was driving a power mower that was as big as their old brown pick-up truck parked by the road. The truck was missing half of a rear fender. They were going to need help when they tried to load that mower into the back of the beat-up pick-up truck. Gardening must not pay as well as I thought in this rich neighborhood. Louella's Mercedes was parked in the garage. The other stall was empty. I wonder if Louella is having her own illicit affair behind Lawrence's back, but I haven't found much evidence and it was really none of my business. The Lafontes were just another of our town's warm happy families.

I walked back to my car—I was due at JJ's office in a half hour.

17

The morning newspapers were scattered about JJ's desk. They'd forgotten about their voodoo explanations and had done a bit of research. James Alexander was a teaching assistant at Toulouse College, an engineering school a couple of hours to the north. He was a handsome young man, about twenty-eight years old, but the published photograph was not up to date—it was dredged up from an old high school yearbook. He had no close living family members, which, given the way he died, seemed fortunate. The reporters were not to be discouraged, however, and they found a distant cousin who was eager to talk about Jim's good and bad qualities, even though she hadn't seen him since he was fifteen. The enthusiastic coverage drew me in, and I didn't hear JJ return from lunch.

"Good afternoon, Blue. What brings you here? Wait, let me guess. You'd like a police escort to an old pipe factory so you can pick up something that you inconveniently left there."

"Close, but no cigar. Take a look." I handed JJ a copy of the card.

JJ looked at it skeptically, opened it and read it. "To Larry Lafonte. Hmm. I think we'd better bring Chief MacGregor in on this." I liked that idea—anything that included Chief Mac-

Gregor made my life better. He lifted his phone, punched in a

number, and spoke with the Chief.

"She'll be down in a minute." JJ read the back of the card again, tapping his fingers on the desk.

" I hid it in one of the pipes," I explained. "Had to get it out before they carted them all away, and the guard wasn't letting me on the site. Thanks to you, here it is."

"I helped you get a letter that could ruin a guy's career," JJ said. "Not sure what I accomplished with that move."

Kathy opened the door and came in. "What's up, JJ?" I looked at her soft brown hair. She looked at me, smiled, then quickly got down to business.

JJ handed the card to Kathy. She sat down and slowly read it, then asked, "Who's Sweetie?"

JJ looked at me. I shrugged. "Guess the main suspect is Vera Bishop. She's disappeared. Called in to KittyLuv to say she was taking some time off, and that's the last anyone's has heard from her."

"Okay, Mr. Heron." Kathy leaned back and folded her arms behind her head. "You'd better fill us in, from the beginning."

For the next twenty minutes JJ and Kathy sat quietly while I ran through the story. Hired by Louella Lafonte, then checking on KittyLuv, meeting Vera. I could see Kathy was skeptical that Vera had picked me up in the bar, rather than the other way around. I described the events at the Pipe Factory. It wasn't a bad story, and I got into the drama of it as I went along. I was tempted to act out the last scene, running through the forest in the dark, with a steel pipe, while bullets thudded into the tree trunks around me.

"We're not buying the movie rights, you know," Kathy said with a note of sarcasm.

JJ stepped in. "Blue, you didn't mention Vera and the guy who shot the door down."

"Oh, it didn't seem relevant at the time," I replied.

JJ and Kathy looked at each other.

JJ shook his head, laid both hands palms down on his desk, and began his analysis. "We have a letter here, to Lawrence Lafonte, on a KittyLuv card. Suggests a hot affair is going on between Sweetie and Mr. Lafonte, the respected, church going, good Samaritan, lover of kittens. If this letter hits the press, Lafonte and KittyLuv have a lot to lose. Donations would drop off drastically. People who save kittens don't like sordid sexual affairs. Apparently somebody knew that Miss Bishop had the letter and is willing to break a few laws to get it back. On the other hand it doesn't add up that she is the one having the affair and wrote the letter. If that were the case, there be a lot of ways for her to reveal the affair, and the letter wouldn't be particularly important. Somebody else wrote it, and Miss Bishop either found it or it was given to her."

"So," Kathy interrupted. "The first thing is to make sure this is kept confidential."

"Ahh," I started to add, then stopped.

Kathy glared at me. "Blue. You didn't!"

"Well, actually, this is a copy. I gave the original to Louella Lafonte."

Kathy exploded. "What were you thinking? For Christ's sake, Blue, reputations, if not lives, are at stake here."

"I'm a private detective. I was hired to do something and I did it. That's my job." I looked at Kathy. "You want me to have a job, right?"

Kathy turned to JJ. "Do you see any laws broken here? Give me some excuse to lock this guy up for a few days."

I tried to defend myself. "Mrs. Lafonte doesn't want to publicize this. She made me promise not to tell anyone else. I'm violating the detective-client privilege just by sharing this with you guys."

JJ snickered. "Detective-client privilege. Which constitu-

tional amendment was that? I forget."

I went on. "Louella will no doubt show it to her husband and they will get divorced, and she'll get a good settlement. That's essentially what she wants. His reputation can weather that."

Kathy was calming down. "I'm worried about Miss Bishop's safety. We should track her down and offer help if she needs it. Blue, you say she hasn't been at KittyLuv since she was chased."

"I have a source watching the place. He hasn't seen her. She has an apartment in the city," I offered.

Kathy went on. "Something else troubles me here. The guy who was killed on the tracks. The coroner says that happened Tuesday evening, not long after you saw him in the Coliseum Bar, and close to the time the gunman is shooting up the door in the Pipe Factory. The dead man had no identification on him. JJ, what else did you find out?"

JJ referred to a report on his desk. "His name is James Alexander, twenty-eight years old. Grew up out West, but has lived for quite a while in North Mansfield, where he teaches, ah taught, at Toulouse College. As far as we can tell his parents are dead, which is probably a blessing. The coroner says there was no sign of drug use, no bruises or marks that didn't match the idea that death came from the train wheel, but he believes it's more likely that he was strangled and then laid on the tracks. We'll know more after the results come in from the lab."

"What about the backpack?" I asked.

JJ looked through the report. "Couple of books, engineering texts, a note pad, pen, pencil, and, this is odd, a trowel."

"A trowel?" Kathy repeated.

"Yes. Standard garden trowel. Maybe the guy liked to garden. You know anything else?" JJ looked at me.

"Maybe, " I said. "I'm curious about the demolition crew. They were hired by Diamond Realty, a big-time real estate firm in New York. One of their guys was at the Buildings Department the day after JJ shut them down, looking for a permit."

"They get one?" JJ asked.

"No. Turns out they don't own it. Tried to slip Charles a few bucks to get the permit, but Charley decided to get honest for the moment. The Pipe Factory and the land it sits on are owned by Vera Bishop, but . . ."

"But what?" Kathy and JJ said in unison.

"An option exists to buy the place. Mr. Bishop apparently needed some money. The factory was slowly dying, and he was going broke, so he negotiated a loan and gave the right to buy the place as collateral if he didn't repay the loan within ten years. It was never acted on, and Vera still owns everything."

"Who holds the option to buy?" Kathy asked.

"Larry Lafonte," I said with a smug sense of having found out something important. But they both looked at me with puzzled expressions.

"So. What does that mean?" JJ asked. "Is Miss Bishop trying to sell the place?"

"No. Not at all. Wants to turn the place into an industrial museum in honor of her father."

JJ scratched his chin—something was bothering him. "Tell me about KittyLuv, Blue. What's really going on over there? There's a lot of money moving in and out and, judging by their brochures, quite a bit gets sent out of the country."

"What are you thinking? Smuggling drugs in condoms in cats stomachs? Hiring young girls to transport homeless kittens when it's the girls who are really being smuggled in? I don't think so, JJ."

"Blue, you're usually the cynical one. Can't believe you trust them."

"Sorry, but all I see is love for fuzzy things."

"What do you think?" JJ asked his boss. "Should we talk with Mr. Lafonte?"

"Absolutely not." Kathy was firm. "The letter's between him and his wife; none of our business. But I would like to know who Sweetie is."

I remembered my trip through the offices. "KittyLuv is loaded with attractive young sweeties. All suspects at the moment."

"Now that you're unemployed again, sounds like you should apply for a job there," Kathy said with a forced smile.

We sat quietly waiting for someone to suggest the next step. JJ broke the silence. "Blue, have you got a plan?"

"Of course. I thought I'd visit the KittyLuv offices and call out 'Hey Sweetie,' and see who answers."

JJ and Kathy looked at me. JJ asked, "You get paid for this?"

"It's his job," Kathy added. "Blue, do you think that headless scene was meant to scare Miss Bishop, maybe force her to sell?"

I agreed with that theory.

"I'd like to check on the factory. Blue, let's go by there."

"Sure. When?"

"Can't do it until Thursday. We'll go in your car. I'd rather not tip anyone off that the police are looking around the factory. Now I'm back to work." Kathy left without another word, slamming the door as she went out.

JJ smiled at me. "You've got your work cut out for you with that one. She's not the easiest kitten to pet."

18

The name of the town was North Mansfield. Toulouse College was the name of the train station. Toulouse Street was the name of the main street through the small town. There was Toulouse Drug Store, Toulouse Realty, and a Toulouse gas station on the corner. Two small clothing stores featured shirts and jackets emblazoned with Toulouse College and a coat of arms borrowed from the shield of a thirteenth-century French crusader. A small tourist shop featured knickknacks, mugs, and postcards sporting the college symbols. North Mansfield's only reason for existence was the college that pushed against the back of the stores along Toulouse Street.

Two imposing brick pillars framed a drive that rose from the town up a small hill to the main campus. An ornate metal arch spanned the drive; Toulouse was spelled out in black iron letters. The scene was modeled on an Ivy League brochure. Buildings crafted of stone and covered with masses of ivy led up the slope to the main hall, topped with a classic clock tower. Between the buildings lay an endless finely manicured lawn crisscrossed with paved paths that mimicked the destinations of the students. The campus was quiet—a few students lounged on the lawn—normal for a hot August afternoon.

The Engineering School was housed in the only modern building on campus, a six-story glass box on the side of the hill looking as though it had dropped in from outer space. I entered through glass doors in a high glass wall. At the side of the lobby was a makeshift shrine covered with flowers, notes, and pictures. I recognized a large photograph of Jim Alexander in the middle. I tried reading a few of the notes. I'm not a sentimental guy, but I had to turn away.

I spent the next hour and a half wandering through the building. A picture of a kitten on a billboard caught my eye. The poster announced a KittyLuv fundraiser that took place a couple of weeks ago. I talked with any teacher or student I could find. They were all uncharacteristically open and trusting of a guy who just walked in and started asking questions. I learned from a secretary that Jim had been a Ph.D. candidate and a teaching assistant at the school. A professor told me that Jim was a good student and a good teacher. Another told me that Jim's specialty was in strengths of materials, and his thesis was titled something like "The Inherent Strengths and Weaknesses of the Properties of Construction Support Materials." Two students told me that he didn't appear to have had a steady girlfriend and seemed to have no enemies, and then they started to cry. He sounded like a darn nice guy, but people don't tend to talk about the down side of friends who have just met violent deaths.

As I was leaving the building, I stopped to watch a pretty young woman tend to the shrine. She pinned up a few notes that had fallen, straightened the flowers, and weeded out a few that were imitating Jim's mortality. "Very sad, really." I comforted. The young student broke into tears. I handed her a tissue. She sniffed, blew her nose, and pulled herself together.

"He was so nice. It's just not fair."

"Will there be a memorial?" I asked.

"Next week." She pointed to an announcement tacked to the bulletin board. "Friday, at the chapel."

I thanked her and wished her well. Then I asked her where I could get a sandwich and a coffee.

"The campus store is just around back. Follow me, I'm headed there."

I followed her around the side of the building to a make-shift structure that had been awkwardly attached at the side of the clean glass façade. It served as a small coffee-sandwich shop that also stocked basic groceries for students who wanted to eat in their rooms. I ordered a BLT and a black coffee and stood in line behind the young woman who had helped me. "Two coffees?" I asked. "You must be very thirsty."

"For me and my boyfriend. And lunch," she said, pointing at two sandwiches.

"Only two?" I asked, trying to be the friendly stranger. "Then why the box of sandwich bags?"

"Oh, that's for my project," she replied with a smile. "Research paper. I have to get some samples of rotting vegetables to analyze. I know, sounds gross. Have to get to class, see you."

"Good luck!" I called as she hurried back to the glass box. I was impressed at how quickly she recovered from her grief; I was jealous of the resilience of the young.

I took my sandwich and coffee to a bench where I could look down upon the town of North Mansfield. It was hard to imagine how a life as seemingly peaceful and hopeful as Jim Alexander's could be crushed out by the steel wheel of an old dying boxcar. It certainly wasn't a suicide; that wouldn't make any sense. Neither did the idea that it could have been an accident. A kid travels down from an idyllic college just to get drunk and fall asleep in a deserted rail yard using a steel track for a pillow. Apparently the coroner thinks Jim was strangled before being laid on the tracks. The clock on the tower chimed four times. The next train was due at four thirty. I finished the sandwich, drained the coffee, dropped the wrappings in a trashcan, and started down the hill to catch the four thirty. The four thirty to New York; that was the last train that Jim would ever catch.

19

Kathy lived in a quiet green area just out of reach of the so-cial restrictions of Marble Hill. The residents all bragged that they lived in Marble Hill, but the residents of Marble Hill re-fused to be associated with their poorer neighbors and called them "Looney Town." She lived in an apartment in a two-story house on an unpretentious tree-lined street. On both sides a row of single-family homes sat behind well-trimmed lawns, which the August sun was drying to a brownish yel-low. Each clapboard home was separated from its neighbor by a thin walkway, just enough to maintain its identity as a separate house. These were houses built in the fifties to satisfy the American Dream of the growing middle class. I parked on the street, and walked through to the back yard. Wood-en stairs that doubled as a fire escape led to a porch on the second floor. Kathy was waiting, seated on a wooden bench, reading the paper. She was wearing sneakers, bluejeans, and a loose untucked white shirt, about as casually dressed as I'd ever seen her.

"Hi!" Kathy greeted me with a big smile and little of the Chief of Police attitude.

"Morning, Beautiful." I pointed to her outfit. "Are those regulation Police Department issue for plainclothes work?

"They're my disguise." She laughed.

We drove out of the quiet community onto 131, to Lincoln Avenue, and turned onto Corncob Road. No cars were parked in front of the factory, but I didn't want to announce our presence, so I drove to the parking area at the end of the road.

"We can go through the corn field and enter around back," I explained. It was one of those perfect August days. The rain had gone out to sea, the sky was crystal clear, and the bright sun had dried the ground. The corn was as high as the top of my head. We used to call the second harvest "cow corn." The kernels were bigger and tougher than those of the young tender cobs earlier in the summer. The stalks allowed us only to see down the row in front of us, and far ahead the back wall of the pipe factory was visible. We approached carefully, but the place was deserted. The downstairs door was not locked and swung open easily, letting us into the large industrial space. It was quiet and dark even in the middle of a sunny day. I could swear that the machines had shifted positions since my last visit.

Kathy stared at the scene before us. "Looks like a technological Easter Island."

I think the large metal crushing machine winked at Kathy as we started up the stairs. The door to Vera's loft hung limply open on one hinge. Inside, splinters of wood and slivers of metal were scattered about the floor. I didn't need to turn on the light. In the daytime sunlight streamed through the overhead skylights, and I could see for the first time the full extent of the loft. The bookshelves rose up two walls to the ceiling, each with wheeled ladders attached that gave access to even the highest shelf. Kathy just said "wow" and started to scour the place for anything that could lead us to Vera. The historical presence was overwhelming; books, small machines on pedestals, old black-and-white photographs of factories. The wooden drawer still lay on the floor. There was no evidence of Vera's presence.

Kathy started with the kitchen. I pulled aside the curtain to the sleeping area. One narrow bed, well made, a clothes rack against the wall with a few dresses, a summer coat, a couple of pairs of pants. A bureau stood at the end of the bed. The biggest drawer was filled with jeans and shorts, and sweat-shirts. I opened a thinner drawer, which revealed a jumble of frills—panties of many colors, bras that were sizable enough to handle Vera's magnificent bosom, and lacy slips. I resisted the urge to jump in and roll around.

"Find anything interesting?" Kathy was looking over my shoulder.

I pushed the drawer closed and opened the small one on the top. It was filled with papers, old bills, advertisements, phone numbers for a plumber and an electrician. "Not much, except here's the address of her New York apartment." I lifted an electric bill from the pile.

We continued to search, trying our best not to disturb Vera's life, although I doubted she would be back here for a while. If getting shot at is not enough to give one a pretty good reason to clear out, the image of a head separated from the body on a train track should do the trick.

"I've seen enough, although this place is amazing," Kathy said. "The museum idea takes on a whole new meaning when you see this stuff. "

"The New York address is a start—I can follow up on that," I added.

"Show me the back way out, the route Vera took when she ran away."

I escorted Kathy out through the back door and down the fire escape on the side. We walked around to the back of the building. There the Kathy I knew and loved reemerged.

"Race you back!" she challenged, and took off into the cornfield.

I chased her. She ran before me, down the rows between the high cornstalks. She was graceful, darting between the stalks from row to row, feet turning up behind her. Her bottom, even in the loose blue jeans, centered the motion, pumping up and down, pistons to drive the legs. I ran, or galumphed, behind her. She was graceful, I was not, but my legs were longer—my stride greater, and I grabbed her from behind, wrapping my arms around her, cupping her breasts in my hands as we crashed through the cornstalks and fell into the weeds. We rolled back and forth, and crushed corn and weeds, flattening a circle beneath our bodies; a couple of aliens creating a crop circle. In our private bedroom I bent over her and kissed her, or she kissed me, and I searched for the buttons on her shirt. Kathy just pulled on mine, and one button popped off. I thought that I should search for it in the crushed plants. Kathy laughed, and ripped off another one. I managed to undo all her buttons without losing a single one, but found myself blocked by a tight T-shirt. I grabbed at the bottom and pulled it up. She wasn't wearing a bra; her bare left breast looked at me, and it was lovely. An erect nipple, centered in one of Kathy's fine, large-as-silver-dollar aureoles, was inviting me. It tasted divine. Kathy had unbuckled my belt but was still fighting with the zipper of the fly. She leaned back, grabbed the cuffs of my pants and tugged, and fell backwards. I rolled on top of her. Something jumped from beneath us as we crashed down—a frog. A big green curious frog sat next to us, motionless on the grass. I'd never made love while being watched by a frog, and I could see by the expression on his face that he had never watched before. I stared at him. He stared at me.

"Is something wrong?" Kathy sat up.

"Just a frog." I pushed her and she fell giggling into the forest of weeds and cornstalks. I managed to find enough opening between her undone blue jeans and the panties pulled to one side to maneuver inside her. We rocked back and forth, crushing down the cornstalks, creating a muddy spot in the damp earth. The squishing of the mud was rhythmic, musical. A steady beat, a marching band. A steady erotic song. But it's not right; it's a bit off. A second rhythm began to challenge ours. A squishing, with clumsy beats, off-rhythm sound. We both froze—recognizing the sound of approaching footsteps. Boots crunching along the rows, and through the cornstalks.

We heard voices: "Damnit! Where are they?"

"I tell you, I saw 'em. Down here somewheres."

The top of a head bounced along the top of the corn—I recognized the buzz cut. They were only about three rows away, but the corn was thick, and the weeds were thick, and so far we were invisible. For a moment they stopped. I couldn't hear what was said, but I heard the distinct sound of a rifle being cocked. Kathy and I didn't move a muscle. They started walking again and the crunching moved into the distance. We lay together, then Kathy whispered, "Let's get out of here."

"Wait. I'm not done."

"You're not what?"

"In a minute, move your leg a bit." I started rocking against her.

"We were ten feet away from being shot and you're still hard as a rock. Didn't that scare you a bit?" Kathy said with exasperation.

"It frightened the shit out of me, but first things first."

"That's lovely and all, but I'd rather not get shot just for a good fuck." Kathy gave me a hard shove, and I popped out like the cork from a fine bottle of Dom Perignon.

Kathy was grinning as she looked down at me lying in the crushed corn. "Come on, Blue. We've got to get out of here."

"Wait—my pants."

We clumsily pulled our clothes back to semi-decency and began to run down the row in a crouch. At the end of the cornfield we stopped and listened. We stepped cautiously out into the open. No sign of the posse. We hurried back into the Beamer, slammed the doors, and turned the key with one motion. I stepped hard on the gas pedal, the Beamer threw gravel into the corn, and we sped down the road around the corner. We raced by the SUV parked in front of the factory, but no one was in sight.

"That was close." I let my shoulders finally relax. "But Kathy, I really don't understand your priorities." I looked at her. She was a disheveled sight with mud on her jeans, her shirt open, one sock up and one sock down around her ankles, and her brown hair falling over her eyes.

"Dinner tomorrow?" I asked.

"You forget, Blue. I'm seeing someone."

20

Friday morning; the sun was rubbing the sleep out of its eyes when I dragged myself out of bed. Showered, shaved, put on a clean gray suit. Studied the three ties hanging in the closet and picked out a conservative, wide red stripe. A quick cup of instant to assure that my eyes stayed open while I drove to the train. Today I am one of a million commuters planning to take the 7:30 to New York City. I don't see this time of day very often—7:00 is an unholy hour. I was surprised to see that the sun had already risen above the tall maples along Machinist's Drive. The Drive was as deserted as usual, but Route 131 was solid cars and slow going. I crept along, constantly checking my watch. When I turned onto Lincoln Avenue, the traffic came to a virtual halt. With sporadic starts and stops, South Station came into view. As I backed into the last available parking spot at the far end of the lot, the train was pulling into the station. I had to run to catch it. I didn't know the routine, but a crowd of early commuters who had taken this trip thousands of times were running alongside of me.

The train car wasn't full—there were a number of stops between our town and the city, and a throng of early risers would board at each one. I found a seat next to a guy with wires leading from his ears to a small metal glowing card in his hands. I wondered if his head was the battery that pow-ered the device. Judging by my fellow riders, I could choose between reading the morning paper, twiddling my thumbs on one of the little electronic gadgets, or sleeping. I chose sleeping.

We were disgorged en masse at Grand Central Station. The terminal is magnificent, but it is impossible to look up and ap-preciate the starry sky on the ceiling without being trampled. Normal traffic rules gave way to a remarkable working chaos. Each commuter took an individual route across the wide hall in a seemingly random direction that magically avoided col-lisions. I remembered watching a large black ant migration across an open field. Each ant pursued a path of unexplainable movement; skittering this way and that, forward and back, circling around with no idea where he was headed. The entire thousand-ant colony, however, moved in a precise two-by-six-foot carpet, smoothly and steadily in one direction toward a new home. I followed the colony that I had become part of and was ejected from the station onto Forty-second Street. I stood to one side, got my bearings, and began walking to Lexington to catch a bus downtown.

I hadn't been to the city for a couple of years, but every-thing seemed strangely familiar. Unfamiliarly familiar. The same old unfamiliar faces. The usual anonymity, the consis-tent diversity, the normally abnormal. The city is home to millions of familiar faces that I've never seen before. The same faces I remember never seeing the last time I was here. In this city even a tall lanky guy, a bit of a hick like me can become invisible. So I try to fit in—to not stand out. The only way to be the same in New York City is to be different, like every-body else.

By the time I get off the bus in the Village, I realize how much I've missed this city. Especially in August, hot, steamy

August when walking in the Village isn't that much different than going to a strip show. I was on Vera's block and I checked in my briefcase for the exact address. Yes, I brought a briefcase. Later today it may be important for me to masquerade as a respectable member of the establishment.

Vera's apartment was on the third floor of a six-story walkup built before Otis and his elevators revolutionized the design of apartment buildings. The front door was locked; the panel showed two apartments on the third floor. Lopez in 3A and Bishop in 3B. Vera didn't answer her buzzer. As I stood in front planning my next move, a teenage boy wielding a skateboard burst through the door and rocketed off down the block. I caught the door before it closed and took the stairs to the third floor. I knocked on 3B—no answer. I pounded harder, and the door to 3A opened. A short, round Mrs. Lopez poked her head out.

"Can I help?"

"I'm looking for Vera Bishop. She doesn't seem to be around. I'm a friend, do you know her?"

"Of course. But she's away."

"Do you now where I can find her? Maybe she'll be in if I come by later."

"I don't think she'll be back soon. She left in a rush. Asked me to water her plants, so I think she may be away for a few days, at least."

Mrs. Lopez wasn't the suspicious type, so I pressed a bit. "I'm worried about her. Haven't been able to contact her. She seems to have disappeared. When did she leave here?"

"Vera knocked on my door late at night. I think it was the Tuesday before last, almost midnight. She asked me to look after her place and gave me a set of keys. She had a suitcase, so I asked her where she was headed. She just shook her head, thanked me, and off she went down the stairs." Mrs. Lopez frowned. "Do you think something has happened?"

"I don't know. Has anybody been around looking for her?"

"There's this older guy, with the bushy eyebrows. But I haven't seen him for a while." Mrs. Lopez thought for a moment. "Another guy, a big fellow, came by just the other day. I heard him knocking, but Vera wasn't home. I didn't talk to him. I didn't like what I saw through the peephole, so I stayed inside."

"That's strange. I wonder . . ." I left the sentence hanging.

"I'll tell you what's strange," Mrs. Lopez said. "Wait a second." She stepped back into her apartment and came back holding a doll. "I found this, over in the corner of the hall, behind Vera's door."

I took the doll from her. It was a classic Barbie Doll, with too-long legs, and oversized breasts, and . . . she didn't have a head.

I thanked Mrs. Lopez and told her I doubted that Vera would be back soon and assured her that Vera would appreciate her watering the plants. I gave her my phone number and asked her to call if she learned anything. Vera was clearly on the run, but where? I was relieved that she wasn't trying to stay in the apartment.

Next stop—my avatar, Mr. George Von Brecker, has some work to do.

21

A brownstone on East Forty-third Street was gasping for air between two forty-story glass office buildings. A sign planted in the space between the building and the sidewalk proclaimed DIAMOND REALTY—DEVELOPMENT PLANNING. I walked up the curving stone steps and entered a small foyer. I pushed the buzzer next to the post office boxes on the wall. The inside door buzzed back and I pushed it open. The interior had been gutted and remodeled. The rich history that filled the walls of New York brownstones had been eviscerated and replaced with the same sterile modern office design that filled the two office buildings cradling the brownstone. The interior walls had been removed and the downstairs was one long room, a troubling thought considering that the interior walls in a brownstone were load bearing. Hopefully some steel beams had been inserted between the floors. A receptionist sat at a desk alongside the stairs to the second floor.

I handed her my card, the card that read:

Mr. George Von Brecker
Investment Consultant

I'd found that "Investment Consultant" covered every area of expertise that I ever needed.

"I'd like to talk with someone about acquiring some properties."

"Of course. Which are you interested in?" The receptionist answered in that maddening accent that ended every sentence on an upswing.

"The rail yards up north," I said as though I knew exactly what I was talking about.

She looked puzzled, started to speak, then stopped and pushed a button on her intercom. "Mr. Jones, there's a gentleman here who wishes to talk about some properties. You might be interested." She got the okay and pointed to the stairs. "Mr. Jones will speak with you. The office is at the front."

The bay windows in the front of the building gave Mr. Jones a nice view of Forty-third Street. The three other walls were covered with maps, development plans, and building designs. Mr. Jones's project was the development of Hope Plaza. I recognized the site. The maps showed the rail yards that I looked over from my fire escape. No tracks were shown on the maps. There were renderings of curving roads and cul-de-sacs, carved up into five-acre building plots. A large area in the center featured a central shopping mall surrounded by a park, which I suspected would actually end up as a massive parking lot. The development extended from South Station to the foot of the hill below the Arms and covered Corncob Road, the old factories, and my favorite cornfield. There were no signs of the old existing buildings on the plans. Large drawings on the far wall showed huge houses, with one-, two-, and even three-car garages, with turrets, and sculptured gardens. Hope Plaza was intended to appeal to those who had worked long and hard for success and wanted to buy a place that would convince their neighbors and themselves that they had succeeded.

Mr. Sidney Jones, as announced on a plaque on his desk, rose to greet me. He looked at the card I handed to him and cheerily opened with, "What can I do for you, Mr. Von Brecker?"

Sidney matched my real estate broker stereotype. Average height, average build, clean but unassuming suit, shined shoes, and an ingratiating smile. His suit coat hung over the back of his chair, his tie was loosened just enough, glasses parked on top of his black hair, cut with just enough gray to add some distinction. A Mont Blanc pen poked out of his breast pocket.

"I'll get right to the point, Mr. Jones. I'm sure you're a busy man, and I don't want to waste your time. I represent some clients who would like to get in on Hope Plaza right from the beginning."

"Where did you hear about Hope?" Jones asked suspiciously. But his chest swelled, and he couldn't resist bragging about his project. "It's going to be big—the biggest thing in the area, but we haven't gone public yet."

"Marcus told me."

"Marcus?" Jones repeated and didn't ask me for a last name.

"Lot of money to be made there," I said with the conspiratorial grin of one real estate guy to another.

"It's my baby," boasted Jones. "What's your line?"

"My clients would be willing to put down a chunk of money on a number of the best sites."

"It'll be out there by November. I could talk to your clients about it then." Mr. Jones was delaying. Diamond Realty hadn't secured the deal yet.

"I'm the one to talk with," I pressed him. "But I don't want to wait until November. You give me an early price, and I give you money—cash—up front. Gives you the bragging rights of rapid sales. A 'get-em-before-they're-gone' advertizing campaign. Gives my guys a better price. We both win."

Jones liked this kind of talk. "Sounds like we could work out something. What can you offer?"

"I'd need a guarantee that the project will come off as planned. That you've got the land, the rights, and such."

"We've got the rail yards sewed up. No problem."

"What about those old factories up Corncob Road?"

"We got 'em. Not a problem," Jones said confidently.

"Even that big clunker, the Bishop Pipe Factory? I noticed that it is still in the name of a Miss Bishop."

Jones frowned. "I see you've been doing your research, George. Don't underestimate us; we'll have the factory. Don't worry."

"But what will you do with the KittyLuv guy? I hear he could buy it at a real nice price." I didn't wait for Jones to answer. "I have clients that will go for twenty or twenty-five lots, depending on the price, but you've got to assure me that the project is going ahead."

"You're talking about small problems." Jones grinned. "I'll have it sewed up by the end of next week. But I'll need some solid collateral from you, some financial background. You can't keep your clients' names confidential forever. We have to know where the money comes from. At least to some degree, if you know what I mean."

Nothing like the mention of big bucks to warp the judgment of a slimy real estate broker. I could see the glimmer of money in Jones's gray eyes. "Of course, of course." I waved it off. "These guys are big—you'll be surprised."

I shook Jones' hand, as though we'd just signed a contract. "Can I take a few of these?" I pointed to a pile of brochures on the desk.

"They're not ready for release yet, but if you keep them to yourself, go ahead. Price will jump as soon as the word is out."

I unsnapped my briefcase, carefully turning it away so Jones couldn't see that it was empty, and slipped in a few brochures. I turned to go, and found myself looking into a familiar face, not one that I wanted to see. The big bruiser of a guard who I faced off with at the Bishop Factory was staring at me. He fit the only name I knew him by, Knockout. Time for me to get the hell out of here.

"Excuse me," I stepped around him. "Talk to you later, Sidney." I quickly hit the stairs.

"Hold it!" Knockout yelled, but Jones motioned for him to cool it. KO sputtered something to Jones, which caused Jones to call out. "Just a second. Come back here!"

I was at the bottom of the stairs when KO came thundering down after me. I would have made it out, but the postman was in the passageway at the entrance, the mailboxes were open, and his cart blocked the door. KO grabbed the back of my jacket and spun me around. He yelled in my face, "What the fuck are you doing here?"

Jones was right behind him. "What are you up to, Brecker? What kind of game is this?" His face was bright red. He was used to playing the scammer, not the scammee.

"This is the guy who called the cops on us at the factory. I told Jake that I'd take care of him."

I held up my hand. "No harm. I'm just researching the situation."

At that point Knockout lost it. My hand slowed his fist down, but it still glanced off my cheek and I spun into the mailman, who had been stuffing mail into the boxes and attempting to ignore us. KO's second swing caught his coat sleeve on a mailbox door, and the material ripped all the way to his shoulder. I took advantage of the time he took to un-tangle himself, leaned down, and drove my shoulder into his chest. KO, Jones, and the unlucky postman fell into a heap in the small entranceway. I shoved the postal cart over the squirming mass, making enough room to open the outer door. I tripped on the way down the front steps and fell onto the sidewalk, landing on the briefcase and scattering brochures about the concrete. I jumped up, ready to run, when someone said, "Are you okay?"

I've never really been fond of the New York City police, but I immediately fell in love with the uniformed officer standing in front of me. I looked back to see Jones and KO standing in the open door. Jones had his hand on KO's shoul-der, holding him back. The unfortunate postman was peering out from behind.

"I'm fine. Just tripped. But that does hurt." I held my knee. I gathered up the brochures and put them back into the crushed briefcase.

"You're sure?" the officer asked. "You're bleeding. I can call for help."

I checked my cheek and came away with a bloody finger. "No, but thanks anyway. Just bruises. I don't have far to go. I'll be okay." I looked again at Jones and his bodyguard. I could see that Jones did not want the police involved in this. He and Knockout stood silently glaring at me. "Thanks, guys." I waved to them. "Don't worry, I'll be fine. See you soon." I turned to the officer. "And thanks again, sir." I forced the briefcase closed and hurried off down the street.

I turned the corner to Grand Central Station, limping, carrying a crushed briefcase, with a bloody cheek, and no one gave me a second look. I love this city.

. . . .

My trip to the city left me in need of the weekend to recuper-
ate. I slept in, then called KittyLuv. I was able to convince
Sybil that I needed to see Larry Lafonte Monday morning,
and she set up an eleven a.m. appointment. A suggestion that
one might be a rich donor can open many doors. I spent the
rest of the day wandering around the Internet, checking on
Diamond Realty, and, of course, KittyLuv. Benny had already
scoped out most of the sites and I didn't learn anything new,
except that cute pets had replaced porn as the subject of the
most popular sites on the web.

22

I picked up two coffees on the way to the Park. Number Six was reliably in place on his bench. I sat down next to him and held out a coffee. He looked at it as though I were handing him a cup of hemlock, but then reluctantly accepted my offering.

"Seen the redhead?" I asked.

He shook his head.

I watched the long black limo pull up in front of the KittyLuv headquarters. Samson got out, took a cloth from the trunk, and searched for any small piece of dust that he could wipe away.

"I think I should say hello," I said to no one in particular.

"The fucker," Number Six mumbled.

Six stared straight ahead. He was sipping the coffee. I had just hired an assistant. I walked down the slope and stood by the limo. "Excuse me, Mr. Wheatley?"

Samson looked up from his polishing. "Yes, but you can call me Sam, or even Samson. That's what my friends call me."

"Samson. That explains the long hair."

The chauffeur laughed, and self-consciously brushed his sandy hair back from his forehead. "I've seen you around.

You have business with Mr. Lafonte?" Samson asked, his eyes dropping for just a second to my crotch.

"Yes, sort of. I'm actually a friend of Vera Bishop. Haven't been able to reach her for a while—I was wondering if you had seen her."

"No. She hasn't been in recently. Maybe on vacation. I don't know."

"Okay. Just asking." I wanted to keep the conversation light.

"Have you asked around the office? They should know." Samson offered helpfully.

"I'm going to see them now. I have an appointment with Mr. Lafonte."

"Good luck." Samson smiled again.

"By the way. What have you got against the guy on the bench?"

Samson looked up at Number Six. "You mean the smelly tramp?"

"Looks harmless to me," I said.

"He's a nuisance. When the wind blows the wrong way you can smell him all the way down here, but the cops won't let me kick him out. Not good for our image to have a scumbag in the front yard."

"I see what you mean, I guess." I agreed, sort of.

Samson stared at Six and rolled back a sleeve as though he was about to start a fight.

I understood why Six referred to Samson as "the fucker." I turned to go. "Thanks, Samson. And I hope you feel better."

"What? I feel fine."

"Just that the nasty bruise on your arm looks painful. Anything broken?"

Samson stared at me, then tried to explain. "No. Just caught it in the car door. It'll be okay."

I left Samson and crossed to the KittyLuv entrance. Just before the door closed behind me, I looked back. Samson had rolled up the other sleeve and was staring at me.

. . . .

I arrived on time for my appointment to see Mr. Lafonte. Sybil greeted me with a puzzled look, no doubt wondering why I wasn't holding a homeless cat. She held her tongue and said Mr. Lafonte was busy at the moment. It might be a few minutes, so if I could please wait. She pointed to a chair off to the side. I sat obediently and surveyed the office. Still no sign of Rose and Betty at their desks. The windows looked out on to the Park, and I could see Number Six sitting on his bench. His redheaded fantasy hadn't shown up for over a week, and I expected he was quite unhappy about the loss. A warm summer breeze blew in through the window, fluttering the curtains and Sybil's loose dress. The fabric floated upward about her, revealing quick glimpses of leg, knee, and white thigh, leaving tempting hints of what might still lie hidden beneath. As I watched, the breeze picked up and lifted the gauzy fabric away from Sybil and into the air. She jumped up from her desk and began chasing the elusive material about the room. She had forgotten to wear anything under her dress, and her naked body gracefully leaped about the office, trying to catch the ghost of a dress. Her breasts, glistening white, swung from side to side, pearly red nipples hanging on for dear life. Sybil stretched her long legs and jumped from desk to desk, but the dress floated just beyond the reach of her fingers. Just as I thought she would float out the window in pursuit of her clothes, Sybil spoke to me.

"Mr. Lafonte will see you now."

"Oh, thank you, Sybil. I'll see you on the way out."

Lafonte's office was in the rear of the building. A large office with windows that faced eastward looking over the buildings in back to a fine view of the low hills at the edge of town. The side walls were covered with pictures of kittens, of people holding kittens, and kittens snuggling with other kittens. The man himself sat in an armchair with only a small desk beside him. Framed commendations, awards, and letters of personal thanks from celebrities, winning athletes, and political figures hung on the wall behind him. He stood, took my hand, and greeted me warmly. The homey, trusting atmosphere made me wish I could escape to the Park and sit with Number Six on his bench. Mr. Lafonte's phone rang. "Excuse me, Mr. Heron, I have to take this call. Please, make yourself at home." He pointed to a chair by the window.

I stood by the double doors that opened onto a terrace— the doors were open, allowing a soft breeze to blow in. I enjoyed the fresh air and the view while Lafonte wooed a perspective donor on the phone. He spoke softly and didn't force the issue. I could sense he was seducing her.

As I looked at the marble terrace, I thought of my rusting fire escape and was tempted to settle in one of the garden chairs, put my feet up on the stone balustrade, and order a martini. A stairway led down from the side, squeezed between the KittyLuv building and the two-story garage in back. It was a back exit and a rather classy fire escape. There was a landing one floor below with a door on one side to the first floor of KittyLuv and on the other to the apartment above the garage. The stone stairs ended unceremoniously in the parking lot below. A few cars were packed in tightly, leaving a space in front of the garage, which was reserved for the limousine. Parked against a fence on the far side of the small lot was a brown Ford pick-up truck, a trailer hitch fastened to the back bumper, and a left rear fender that was only half there. I knew those lawn guys couldn't fit their big mower in that truck, and KittyLuv doesn't even have a lawn. What the hell is the garden crew doing here?

Lafonte interrupted my thoughts. "Mr. Heron. You told Sybil that it was important for you to see me. So, please, what is on your mind?"

I started with the easy part. "I'm a friend of Vera Bishop. She doesn't answer her phone. She's not at her New York apartment, and I gather she has not been to work here either. Frankly, I'm worried about her."

Mr. Lafonte shook his head. "I wish I had something to tell you. It's very unlike her, but she's always had a private side. I've been thinking of going to the police, but I'm hoping that won't be necessary."

"You were one of the last people to see her when you dropped her off at South Station. About six in the evening, I think."

"Whenever I head in that direction, I drop her off, and sometimes I ask Samson, he's my chauffeur, to take her over if she works late. She takes the train to the city or sometimes stays over at the Factory. Seems a bit lonely, but she likes the place."

"Do you charge her rent?" I asked innocently.

"What are you talking about?" Mr. Lafonte's full eyebrows lowered and a cloud crept across his normally calm features.

"I understand you have an option to buy the Factory, and I thought maybe you had, that's all," I said, making it sound as unimportant as I could.

"Mr. Heron, I don't know what you're after. I don't know who you are, but you have no right to question me this way. You're implying that I had something to do with Vera's disappearance. You have no right." A gleam of recognition crossed his face. "And I don't know what the stunt with that alley cat was last week."

"I'm a private investigator. Unfortunately that means I get paid to find things out. You had some kind of fight with Vera

Bishop on the way to South Station. Then she gets chased out of her loft at the Factory by some gun-wielding thug." I stopped to let it sink in.

"Are you crazy!' Lafonte sputtered. "What do you mean she was chased away? You're making this stuff up, and I don't like it. Not one bit!"

"I thought maybe you sent someone after her?"

"For what, to do what!" Lafonte was crimson and probably would have hit me, if he was that kind of a guy.

"To retrieve this," I said as I held my copy of the infamous letter.

Lafonte recognized it immediately. "You! You're the devious snoop! You're the one who gave it to Louella."

"She's talked to you about it?"

"Talked isn't the right word. She thinks this letter will ruin me. She's says she wants a divorce and cash, or the letter goes straight to the papers. But she can't prove the letter isn't a fake—I can fight it. She can have the divorce, but I'll be damned if I'll throw in a big settlement. Now," Lafonte paused and stared at me, "now you want to blackmail me. I think the police should know about this." He reached for the phone.

Mr. Lafonte had not asked me where I found the letter— he knew that Vera had it. "Vera told you she had the letter on the way to the station, didn't she?" I waited. Lafonte didn't pick up the phone. "You're right, I am a snoop. That's my business—private eye. But," I tried to reassure him, "no blackmail, I promise you. I don't really care what's in the letter, or who Sweetie is. That's between you and your wife. But I do want to find Vera, and if I have to use the letter to get your help, I will." We sat in silence. Lafonte glared at me.

"What do you want to know?" he hissed. He forced the words out without moving his lips.

"About the option to buy. Where did that come from?"

"Nothing wrong with that." Mr. Lafonte was relieved not to talk about the letter. "William Bishop, Vera's father, and I were friends from way back. Went to college together, I knew him well. He got in financial trouble; the Factory was failing, and he needed some money. I lent him some, and he gave me the right to buy the Factory as collateral. I never cashed in. Didn't want to. Vera is like a daughter to me. She wants the place and I won't throw her out. Poor guy. He died before his time, but he loved Vera. He'd want her to keep the Factory and turn it into a museum. There, does that answer your question?"

"Did you know James Alexander, the man who was killed on the tracks?"

Lafonte shook his head. "No. What a tragedy."

"You hosted a fundraiser at Toulouse College a couple of weeks ago. Mr. Alexander worked at the college."

"Really?" Lafonte was puzzled. "Never met him."

"Any of your staff go up there with you?"

"Of course. Vera, Thalia, and Marcus." He said the last name with a sigh.

Mr. Lafonte had resigned himself to answering questions, so I kept on. "Do you know Diamond Realty?"

"I've heard of them," Lafonte said tightly.

"They want the Factory and the land around it for a big development, and I have a feeling they get what they want."

Lafonte was quiet.

"You could buy the place and sell it to them. Vera couldn't stop you."

"I'd never do that to Vera."

I was striking a nerve. Lafonte's hands were trembling. I kept going. "If you executed the option, bought the place, then sold it to Diamond Realty, you could make a bundle, yes?"

Lafonte's eyes were burning a hole through my head. "Get out of here, before I call Fitzhugh."

"Diamond Realty seems to think they have you in their pocket. I'd like to know why."

Lafonte reached for the intercom.

"I will find out, Mr. Lafonte. One way or another."

Lafonte leaned down and spoke into the intercom. "Sybil, could you call Fitzhugh. Right away! We have a problem here."

I left Lafonte sitting motionless in his soft chair, staring straight ahead and breathing hard. I believed him when he said he didn't want to harm Vera. I believed him when he said he didn't want to buy the Factory. Sidney Jones knew something about KittyLuv, and he thought it was powerful enough to force Lafonte to buy the Factory and then turn it over to Diamond Realty. I felt sorry for the guy. But when I saw Fitzhugh standing by Sybil's desk, I felt sorry for myself. He was a half-foot taller than I was and could have lifted the desk over his head with one hand. What joker named this Frankenstein impersonator Fitzhugh Botsby?

My fears vanished when he asked Lafonte, "Shall I show the gentleman out, sir?" I should have known that anybody named Fitzhugh would have an English accent.

Mr. Lafonte nodded and Fitzhugh took my arm.

"I know the way. I'm going," I said. I walked around the towering bodyguard, winked at a distressed Sybil, and headed down the stairs. Samson was still standing by the limousine. He watched me closely as I crossed the street to the Park and started up the hill. I didn't look back, but walked to the bench and sat down next to Number Six. Cat-Meow had returned, and came out from under the bench to rub against my leg.

"Don't worry, Six," I said, both of us looking straight ahead. "I'm sure I can find red-top. We'll get her back."

23

LeRoy's Bar and Strip Club doubled as the office for John Heron—Private Investigator. I thought about asking LeRoy if I could put up a sign outside. The office was located just off the Park, near the Courthouse, the Police Station, municipal offices, and KittyLuv. I could check on my reliable surveillance expert, Number Six, any time I wished. Refreshments were available; a beer, a martini and even a bite to eat any time of the day. There was LeRoy, sympathetic and always interested but never too probing. And of course, there's the strip club downstairs. Today, I was waiting to meet Louella Lafonte. She had called and set up another appointment.

I arrived at LeRoy's a few minutes before Louella was due and took the opportunity to bring him up to date. "Greetings friend. I'm meeting my boss again."

LeRoy looked interested. It was a skill that came of years of bartending. "So Blue, how's the case going? Any breakthroughs?"

"Not bad, so far. Pay's good."

"Looks like you're holding up pretty well with a steady job. It's been a couple of weeks now, hasn't it?"

"Almost. I took last weekend off. Can't work all the time."

LeRoy nodded sympathetically. "Did you notice this strange story in *The Herald* this morning?" He pushed the paper across the bar.

A hunter, John McPhee, while searching for pheasants in the cornfield behind the Bishop Pipe Factory, had chanced upon a small crop circle crushed into the stalks. An expert, who had studied the crop circles discovered in England, said that although no one knows exactly how these events came about, it would have had to have been a very small flying saucer to create the circle that McPhee found. LeRoy was enjoying this. "So now we have aliens on the scene."

"Seems like something very strange must have happened out there," I added.

A streak of sunlight announced Louella's arrival. "Here she comes now. Could you bring me a draft and a glass of chardonnay for the lass?" I met Louella by the back table and reached out to take her hand. She ignored the gesture, rubbed the table down with a napkin, and sat down.

"How's the divorce coming along?" I asked, trying to start with idle chatter.

"I need some more details," was Louella's curt response. "He's being stubborn, says the letter is a fake." LeRoy arrived with the drinks. Louella waited until he was out of earshot. "My lawyer tells me I need a name. Just who is Sweetie? I need something solid, some pictures, a recording of a phone call. Something the bastard can't deny."

"Sweetie is more invisible than I had counted on, but I will be able to run her down."

"Can't you follow Vera, tap her phone or something?"

"Mrs. Lafonte, I'm quite sure it's not Vera you're looking for. That relationship is more like father and daughter."

"If you say so," Louella answered with a skeptical roll of the eyes, "but it still looks pretty suspicious to me. If it's not

Vera, then who is it? How about that Sybil girl? Or Rose? I'm paying you well, Mr. Heron. I want something solid."

"It might take a bit of time before one of them makes a mistake, but it will happen and I'll be watching."

"I can wait a bit, but the sooner the better. Keep me informed."

"Mrs. Lafonte, before you go, just a piece of advice. When you hire someone to dig up dirt, the results are often more than you bargained for."

Louella frowned at me. "What are you talking about?"

"I'm talking about uncovering affairs and that people in glass houses shouldn't throw stones."

Louella stood and looked me in the eye. "Just stick to your job, Mr. Heron."

The meeting was over. Louella finished her wine and left me sitting in the quiet bar. Sleuthing isn't the cleanest work in the world. Everybody is hiding something, sometimes from themselves. Larry Lafonte is involved in an affair, and I suspect Louella is also seeing someone on the sly. That pick-up truck is a puzzle—first at the Lafonte estate, then at Kitty-Luv. It's not what I've been hired to do, but I think I'll track it down.

24

I lay in bed listening to the mating sounds of summer. An insistent bird repeated his plea for attention with an annoying triple squeak—no wonder she wasn't answering. A mourning dove cooed seductively, and replies came from two directions. The cicadas and tree frogs were sleeping in—their raucous symphony would begin later in the day. I watched a large, hairy garden spider crawl up the wall by the bed, and thought of Marcus. Doctor Dollar had seen him in some sleazy dealing. He's the head of KittyLuv accounting, yet his photo wasn't included with the staff picture. I'm guessing he's a recent addition. He has some connection to Diamond Realty, as he showed up at the Buildings Department with Jones. Vera, Marcus, and Thalia worked in the same office. I have to learn more about the hairy-eared one. The garden spider jumped off the wall and landed on the side of the bed. It was time for me to get up, which I did rather quickly. I lost track of the eight-legged guy in the sheets. Hopefully he has better things to do and won't be hanging around when I go to bed tonight. Maybe Thalia could tell me something about Vera, and also Marcus.

I didn't need a coffee to wake me; Mister Spider had done that. I found the KittyLuv brochure, and clicked the number of the accounting office into the cell phone. The conversation was short. Thalia was a good friend of Vera's, and was worried that she hadn't been to the office. She was eager to talk with someone about her. We agreed to meet after work. I told her I'd wait on the park bench facing the KittyLuv building.

. . . .

I waited on the bench for the KittyLuv workday to end. Number Six had left; I think he was suffering from the absence of his favorite redhead. The offices around the Park were beginning to open their doors and allow the workers to escape. Just as in the big city, there wasn't any pattern to their movements. People walked in every direction on the sidewalks and across the Park. A group waited on the corner for the bus, some drove out from the parking lots behind the buildings, and a few headed for LeRoy's. KittyLuv's front door opened; Samson was the first out. He walked down the drive to the back. I saw Sybil, and maybe Rose, leave. Then the wide-shouldered Thalia emerged. She stood at the edge of the sidewalk looking about, then spotted me on the bench. I tipped my nonexistent hat, and she strode up the hill. Thalia was wearing a tight jacket over a tank top, running shoes, and jeans. The jeans clung to her legs and emphasized some fine thigh muscles. She looked at me with piercing steel-blue eyes.

"Are you Mr. Heron?"

"Yes, that's me. Do you have some time? I'd like to buy you a coffee or a beer."

Thalia laughed. "Now that's a pretty lame pick-up line. I'm sure you could do better."

"What about 'Haven't I seen you somewhere before?'"

Thalia looked at me curiously. "Wait. I have seen *you* some-where before. You're the guy who left the cat on Marcus' desk."

"Oh, I'm sorry about that."

"Don't be sorry. We thought it was hilarious. You should have seen Marcus when he opened his eyes. You would have thought he was being attacked by a tarantula. He jumped out of his seat and screamed like a little girl."

"And he works at KittyLuv?" I liked Thalia's story. "What happened to the cat?"

"The cat? He jumped off the desk and caught up with you in the hall. I looked out the window and watched you running across the park. The cat was right behind you. Made my day." Thalia couldn't suppress a giggle. "But what was going on?"

"I can explain, or, maybe I can't."

"Try."

"Over a beer?"

"Okay. The cat move got my attention. Have you used that one before?"

"No, but I'll remember it. Let's go over to LeRoy's—you know the place?"

"It's our second office." She smiled and we started across the Park.

Rush hour traffic filled the streets. The drivers were tired at the end of the day, and each was alone in his car. Car pools weren't popular. After a day at the office, these drivers want-ed to be alone, at least for the ride home. Most of the cars had been bought in the last couple of years. This wasn't a poor town, and a new car was high on the list, except for the beat-up pick up truck that passed by. Apparently the tall, hand-some driver couldn't afford a limousine of his own. I'll be damned. Samson and Louella. Interesting.

We crossed at the light and followed the after-work crowd into the bar. The space was already crowded, and we needed some privacy. I ordered two draft beers at the bar and asked LeRoy if we could use his office. He slid the glasses across the bar and nodded in the direction of the office door.

"You seem to know your way around," Thalia said as she followed me.

I closed the door behind us and offered Thalia the chair behind LeRoy's desk. She took the offer, dropped her purse on the desk, and pulled off her jacket. The tank top left her arms bare. She settled back into the chair. "I like this," she said. "Makes me feel like I'm asking the questions." She leaned back, and swiveled back and forth. She began to put her feet on the desk, but decided against it. "You're not about to interview me for a position in the strip club downstairs, are you?"

"I wish I could," I sighed. "But I'm not part of the management—just a friend."

"So. Why did you race out of the office the other day?" Thalia waited for my explanation. "I'm listening." She reached for her beer, sending a ripple up her bicep as she gripped the glass.

"Mr. Lafonte had called for the limousine, and Vera was going with him. I followed them to see where they were going."

"Why?"

"It's rather complicated. But I trailed them to South Station. Mr. Lafonte boarded the train for the city. I thought Vera was going with Lafonte, but she didn't take the train. We met by chance in the Coliseum Bar, and I walked her back to her factory—she stays there some nights. She thought she was being followed, and asked me along for protection."

"I don't understand. Why were you following them?"

"I'm a detective. I'm on a case, and it has overlapped with KittyLuv. Can't tell you more, except that I want to make sure that Vera is safe. As you know, she hasn't been to work for days, and hasn't been to her apartment in New York either."

Thalia was trying to make some sense of my story. "Is Vera in danger?"

"Turned out she was right. A guy turned up. I don't know what he wanted, but he was pretty nasty and carrying a gun. I managed to slow him down a bit, and Vera escaped. No one has seen her since. You work next to her, and I thought you might know where she went."

"We thought she was okay. She sent in a message—said she was taking some time off for a family emergency."

"She didn't want you to worry about her."

"Do you know who the guy was who was after her?"

"No, it was dark, and I never got a good look at him."

Thalia hesitated. "Wait a minute. When did this happen?"

"Two weeks ago, Tuesday."

"Wasn't that the same night that the poor guy got his head chopped off on the train tracks? Do you think . . . ?" She quit her thought in mid-sentence.

"I'm sure Vera got away. The intruder scared her, and I think the gruesome murder was also intended to scare her. She's been hiding ever since."

Thalia's voice broke. "Oh, my God. You say you checked her apartment in the city?"

"Yes. She hasn't been back there."

"I don't have any idea where she is. Poor Vera!" Thalia fought back a tear.

"The week before the murder you went on a fundraising trip to Toulouse College. Can you tell me who went along?"

"Mr. Lafonte, of course. And the accounting team: Vera, Marcus, and me. We're in charge of collecting the money.

Turned out they didn't need all three of us—college sites don't bring in much."

"Was Vera with you the whole time? I'm curious who she talked with at the college."

"When we were about to leave, I couldn't find her at first. Then saw her outside talking to a nice-looking fellow. Marcus started teasing her, saying she was trying to get laid on Kit-tyLuv's time. He's such an ass. Vera said it was her business, not his."

"Have you seen the picture in the paper of the guy who was killed on the tracks?"

"No. I'm not going to spend my time reading about nasty murders."

I took out the picture of Jim Alexander that JJ gave me and showed it to Thalia.

She studied the picture. "I'm not positive, but that does look like him." Then the connection sank in. Thalia looked dumbstruck. "Oh, my God! You think Vera had something to do with this?"

"I'm afraid that Vera either thinks that she will be blamed, or that she will be next. I've got to find her before somebody else does."

"I wish I could help. Poor Vera. But I don't know anything else."

"Tell me about Marcus Doolittle."

"You can say that again. Doolittle. Name should be Do Nothing. He's worthless."

"Didn't he just get promoted to chief of accounting?"

"I should have that job. But Lafonte gave it to Marcus, and a nice big raise to go along with it. Who knows? He'd been hired as a low-level accountant, and then after a couple of weeks, he's suddenly my boss."

"Sounds fishy to me. A mediocre, sleazy, opportunistic nobody who spends most of his days playing solitaire or dozing in front of his computer suddenly gets a big raise. Could Doolittle have come across something he could use against Lafonte?"

Thalia fumbled with her sleeve. "Look, I can't tell you KittyLuv's confidential financial details. I can say everything looked legal, but . . ."

Nothing like a "but" to provoke curiosity. "But" must be one of the most explicit words in the English language, but Thalia was not going to explain further.

"What was Do Nothing's relationship with Vera?"

"He liked to tease her, like he was about twelve years old. Teased her about talking to a stranger—accused her of trying to get laid. Teased her about her dreams for a technology museum. He called it a 'home for used sewer pipes.' He said it was a stupid idea, and that she should sell the place. She said it wasn't her decision any more. Somebody had legal first dibs on it. Marcus kept pushing her, but she just told him to fuck off. I think teasing is his way to feel like a man." Thalia was getting angrier with each sentence. "Frankly, he's a pig!"

Marcus Doolittle had just taken a place on my to-do list. I wasn't sure why, but he appeared to have something on Lafonte.

"Thalia, thanks. You've been very helpful. I think I can catch up with Vera before anything happens to her."

Thalia stood up and put her jacket on. "I hope you do. I still don't know who you are, but if you find out anything about Vera please tell me. Poor Vera." Thalia shook her head and pulled herself together. "Now I have a bus to catch."

We left the office and Thalia walked through the bar to the door. She passed two guys who I recognized from the Police Department. One made one of those you're-so-sexy lip-smacking sounds, but when Thalia stopped in her tracks, put her hands on her hips, and stared at him he choked on his beer. She strode out the door.

I was sorry to have upset Thalia, as she was obviously worried about her friend. She didn't know it, but she had told me where I was going to find Vera.

25

The comings and goings of the Lafonte family were beginning to resemble a plate of spaghetti. Louella was barely dressed when I dropped off the famous letter last week. It was Samson's pick-up truck that was parked out back, and I suspect he was the owner of the feet that showed under the door. She is having an affair with her husband's chauffeur, and at the same time she's using Larry's affair to blackmail him. That can work both ways. She's driving down a two-way street and may be on the wrong side of the road. I think I'd better talk to her. There's a damn good chance that this could backfire—affairs have a way of becoming public, especially when people realize there's a private eye digging around.

The summer air was hot and wet. A mist blanketed the town, saturating the warm air and blurring the shapes of the buildings, streets, and fences. Colors were muted, hard edges were softened. Nature's gentle cloak made our town seem safe and harmless. I turned my Beamer off 131 and through the gates that led to Maple Hill. Wealthy areas are named after trees and flowers. The Lafonte mansion came into focus and I stopped in the circular drive. I left the protection of the car, and by the time I reached the front door, my shirt was damp and clinging to my chest. No one answered the buzzer, although I could hear it chime inside the front hall. I was about to try again when I heard a sound. A door slammed somewhere inside. I pushed the buzzer again. Nothing. I tried the door—it was locked. I walked around to the side of the mansion to the patio door. It was also locked. I peered in through the glass. The inside was familiar. Louella and I had met there when I gave her the letter. The room was empty, but the chair by the table lay on its side. One shoe lay abandoned by the door to the hallway. I tried her number on my cell phone. It rang, and I could also hear a tune play inside the house. The ringing stopped, and Louella's voice said "Louella Lafonte is not available at this time. Please leave your name and number after the tone, and she will return your call as soon as possible."

Enough caution—something was not right. The handle of my pistol easily smashed the glass pane of the patio door, and I used the inside handle to swing it open. I stepped over the broken glass on the floor and was in the salon where I'd sat the first time I was here. Everything looked the same, except for the tipped-over chair and a book that lay open on the table. Tenniel's drawing of the fading grin of the Cheshire Cat looked out at me. I looked toward the front hall and saw the black low-heeled shoe lying lonely on the marble floor. I found the other shoe in the adjoining living room, although this one had a foot in it. A curled form was propped against a leg of the dining room table. Her face was toward the wall, but it was clearly Louella. I dropped to my knees, took her shoulder, and turned her over. Louella's eyes stared blankly at me. Her body was warm, but there was no breath, no heartbeat, and a growing circle of blood soaking the front of her blouse, dripping off the handle of the knife that protruded from her chest. There was no saving her, although this must have happened just moments ago. I checked my shoulder holster and listened. Everything was eerily quiet. I laid poor Louella back down and stood over her for a moment. I left her there and quietly began to tour the house. The search turned up nothing, except that the back door was unlocked, and the screen door on the porch was swinging open. The alley in back was deserted. I used the hall phone to dial the police, unlocked the front door, and went back to the dining room. I thought at least I could keep Louella company until the law arrived. I looked down at the crumpled form on the floor. Her blouse was ripped and there was a cut over her eye. A china vase was in pieces on the floor, water and flowers scattered around her body. There had been a nasty fight, and Louella had lost.

. . . .

After a quick study of Louella's lifeless body, the medic announced that the knife had pierced her heart and killed her instantly. The shattered vase, ripped blouse, and cuts confirmed that Louella had fought her attacker before the deadly thrust. Before the body was carried to the waiting ambulance, the police had outlined her form on the floor with chalk. It was hard to imagine that the amorphous shape that remained—a contorted yellow line with a wide red stain in the middle— marked what used to be a living, breathing person.

I was sitting on the swing on the front porch. The convoy of police vehicles, ambulances, and curious neighbors had drifted away. The tape guys were sealing the entrances to the mansion with yellow strips.

Kathy sat down beside me. She was exhausted, but her day wasn't over. "I have to go see Mr. Lafonte. This is the toughest part of my job."

"Send Corbutt?" I lamely suggested.

"No. Can't dump this off on my crew. I've done this before, and no doubt I'll have to do it again. I have to tell him his wife is dead, and as he's a natural suspect, I have to find out where he was this morning." Kathy walked to the waiting squad car. Her pace was unusually slow, her shoulders uncharacteristically curved down. I watched the squad car turn onto the main road. No sirens or blinking lights for Kathy's trip to KittyLuv. I stood on the porch and watched until the car disappeared around the far corner. The air was crystal clear, the mist had risen, and the sun had taken charge. The landscape had been brought back into sharp focus and no longer seemed as harmless as before.

26

The mood in Kathy's office was serious. We were leafing through the morning editions, waiting for JJ to join us. *The Journal* proclaimed: SOCIALITE STABBED. *The Alternate View's* headline—MURDER SPREE CONTINUES—is hoping for more to come. KittyLuv was getting a lot of unwanted publicity. *The Herald* announced: KITTYLUV WIFE FOUND DEAD. The lead story dutifully confirmed that "No connection has yet been established between the two murders and the crop circle found in back of the Bishop Pipe Factory."

JJ arrived with a "Good morning, guys." He had seen it all in the years on the force, and nothing could faze him.

Kathy started us off, skipping the pleasantries. "What have you found out?"

JJ summarized. "There was a fight. Started in the kitchen, moved to the hallway. The knife was a short carving knife— matching a set in the kitchen. There were no fingerprints. Doesn't look premeditated, but the lack of prints is curious. These guys don't usually wipe off prints and leave the knife in place."

"Murderer might be wearing gloves," Kathy suggested.

"Yes, but it's not cold outside, and it really doesn't look like the murder was planned—it wouldn't have been so messy."

"Witnesses?" Kathy asked.

"Nobody. The neighbors were quizzed, but no one had seen anyone come or go from the Lafonte mansion. That's not unusual for Maple Hill—large hedges separate the houses. Road traffic is minimal, and during the day, few people are home."

He looked at Kathy. "Did you find out anything from Lafonte?"

"Bringing him the news wasn't easy, but he took it about as well as he could. There wasn't any love lost between them, but it still was a pretty tough blow. He was upset because the last times they were together were filled with battles. The evening before she died they had a major fight. He was with her in the limo, driving home from a meeting with the lawyers about their divorce. She didn't like the proposed terms of the settlement and blew her top. She told Lafonte that she had lost her patience and was going to the press the next day. He was facing the destruction of KittyLuv, which gave him a pretty good motive for the murder, except that he says he was working at the time. He has an office full of potential witnesses to vouch for him."

"It's strange." I was thinking out loud. Kathy and JJ decided to let me ramble on. "One guy gets murdered on the tracks, and there's some connection to Lafonte. A woman is murdered in her home—Lafonte's wife. Lafonte seems to be the only link between the two murders."

"Except," Kathy sat forward, "for the only other person around who seems to be involved with both tragedies."

"Who are you thinking of?" I asked.

"You," Kathy said. "How the hell do you get mixed up with the only two murders this town has had in the last five years?"

"Everybody has two sides," I protested.

JJ couldn't resist an analysis. "It's Blue's dual personality. On the one hand, he's the detective who finds the letter. On the other, the seducer who saves the princess."

"Seducee," I corrected. "Vera picked me up and nothing ever happened anyway."

Kathy didn't want to hear the details. "We're not getting anywhere. We have no leads on Louella's murder, but it's still early on in that case. We've identified the poor guy on the tracks, James Alexander, and his background, but we don't know what he was doing there. Vera's hiding somewhere; at least I hope she's hiding." The Chief of Police was frustrated. "Let's get working, keep digging, we need something."

I did not want to volunteer anything about Vera. Vera had trusted me and asked me to keep quiet. I wanted to talk with her before the police did. Tomorrow, if my instincts are correct, I'll be with Vera.

27

Thalia tightened the rope around my wrist and tied it to the bed pole. I was naked, hands and feet tied and stretched to the sides of the bed. Thalia was wearing only a pair of black high heels. She knelt facing my toes, her knees pressed to either side of my head, against my ears. I couldn't move—she smiled down at me. Her stomach was a six-pack of muscles, and her breasts pointed straight ahead. I wondered what exercises she did to keep her mammary muscles in such good shape. She bent forward and fingered me. I was looking up between two white marble columns to a thatched roof. I strained my head upward, but was unable to reach the treasure above. Her touch was soft, and . . . I heard a meow? Thalia was placing kittens on my body—warm, fuzzy, mewing little creatures—all over me. The tiny paws padded over my chest and stomach. One rubbed up against me as if I was the stiff leg of a chair. Thalia leaned forward, and I felt a wet tongue. I felt a warm nose, and then I felt a scrape. "Ouch!" A cat's tongue is rougher than sandpaper. Another raspy lick, and alarm bells began ringing. I bolted upright. Thalia vanished, and the kittens scrambled away. I found the alarm and remembered that I had to get up. It would take me over two hours to drive up to

Toulouse College. I needed to be there today—at the funeral for James Alexander.

. . . .

The Toulouse Chapel, The Mother of the Sacrament Holy Church, watched over the campus. The Chapel sat on the side of the hill, its tall steeple pointing proudly to the heavens. An array of lightning rods kept away the devil. The service for James Alexander was already underway when I arrived. I joined a few latecomers to take a seat in the back row. The hall was full of mourners. The deep voice of a black-clad minister was amplified throughout the space by large speakers on either side of the altar. He was proclaiming the mercy and wisdom of an all-powerful God, who had apparently been on a coffee break when Jim's life was ended. The minister was followed by friends and colleagues of Jim's and by members of the college administration, who eloquently, sadly, and even humorously described a beautiful friend. I began to think of dying, and to imagine the wonderful stories the throng of admirers would tell about me, and how much they would have to lie to do so. Jim's coffin was placed in front of the altar. It was closed. I'd have an open coffin, so I could listen to all the people whom I'd insulted, and who didn't like me very much. They would have to stand up and say what a wonderful guy I was, and how they missed me. An open coffin, so I could lie back and listen to the organ fill the hall with rich funereal chords. After the service, sad faces would appear over the edge of the coffin and peer down at me. One after another looking in. The pizza waitress would come by. She wiped her eyes, said, "Sorry, Blue. I guess I missed my chance." And here's LeRoy. "Brought you a martini. I'll leave it right here." Well look who else turned up, Inspector Corbutt. "Hey, Blue.

I hear that when you die you get a hard on. Mind if I check it out?" And Kathy, beautiful Kathy, tears running down her cheeks peering into the coffin. "Just being with you, Blue, makes me feel sexy all over. You were the best lover ever. Blue, maybe, just one last time. I could climb in there." She lifted one leg over the edge of the casket.

I felt a pat on the shoulder. The service had ended; everyone was filing out and a young student wanted to get by me. I stayed back and stood in the last row watching until the familiar face came up the aisle. Vera's head was bowed—a scarf tried to hide her red hair. I touched her arm; she looked up and was visibly startled to see me. I fell in line beside her and we walked into the afternoon sun. It was a funeral; it should be raining. The coffin was being loaded into a parked hearse. We stood side by side as the mourners took their places in the waiting row of cars. The hearse started slowly down the college lane. The line of cars followed obediently behind until the procession dropped over the edge of the hill and left the campus.

I put my hand on Vera's shoulder. "There's a coffee shop behind the Engineering building—let me treat you."

"How'd you know to find me here?"

"You feel terrible about Jim. I didn't think you would miss the funeral."

Vera nodded, and we walked silently around to the back of the Engineering building. Her breasts snuggled into their usual spot against my arm. We didn't talk; enough had been said at the service. The coffee shop was almost full, but we found a table against the back wall. Vera sat. We hadn't spoken of Louella. Vera had been lying low and probably hadn't seen the yesterday's papers. We had just left a funeral, and I didn't think it was the right time to talk about another murder, even though there wasn't any love lost between Vera and

Mrs. Lafonte. I bought two coffees and the cheeriest piece of coffee cake I could find and took them to the table.

I lifted my cup. "To James."

Vera looked at me with tear-red eyes, puzzled. "Just who are you? I can't believe that a guy I picked up in a bar, then dropped into the middle of a shoot-em-up, would come all the way up here just to see me."

"You probably picked up the wrong guy. I'm a private eye. People hire me to dig around and dredge up embarrassing stuff. Kind of a lousy career, I admit, but at least I get to meet pretty women like you."

"Really?"

"You hired James, didn't you? Brought him to the rail yards."

From the look on Vera's face I realized I was a bit too abrupt. She denied everything. "No! I didn't have anything to do with it!"

"Vera, no one's accusing you of murder, but you are involved. My guess is that you met James here when you came up for the KittyLuv fundraiser. You hired him. You talked with him at the Coliseum Bar before he went to the yards."

Vera looked at the floor. "Why would I do that?"

"He was in the engineering school, an expert on metals. He had some plastic bags and a trowel with him when he died."

Vera was quiet.

"He was there to collect soil samples, in a field next to a factory that had been fabricating pipes since the turn of the century. Pipes used to be made out of lead. Lead is a pollutant. Lead is poisonous. A report of lead in the soil could stop Diamond Realty in their tracks. Just the words 'lead pollution' in the papers would deprive Sidney Jones of millions of dollars."

Vera looked up at me. Her big, innocent, blue eyes were filling with tears. "Yes. You're right. I want to keep the Factory. Make a beautiful technology museum. I hired Jim to do the research."

"If you found lead, wouldn't that hurt your plans also?"

"My dad closed that place years ago—no pipes have been made for years. I sent Jim to a drainage ditch. If there was any chance that there was any lead around that would be the spot. Even so, that could be cleared out. It was a gamble." Vera's voice trembled. "A risk I asked Jim to take. I might as well have killed him. Oh my God, what did I do?" She dropped her head and shook with sobs.

"You didn't kill him, Vera. You didn't know what you were up against. The best thing you can do at this point is to help catch the murderer. You need to come back and talk with the police."

"Boo, they'll kill me. I'm afraid."

"You're right to be afraid. Where are you staying? And it's Blue, not Boo."

"I've been moving around. Last night I stayed at The Four Star Motel. It's not that far from the Factory."

I remembered The Four Star Motel—they normally rented their rooms by the hour. I also remembered that it was not a safe place to stay. There was a direct line from the front desk to every hit man in the business.

"The Four Star? That's no good. I know the place—it's too dangerous. Did you drive up here?"

"No, I left my car at South Station and took the train."

"Let me drive you back and we'll go by the motel, pick up your stuff, and I can put you up for the night. Tomorrow we'll go to the police. I know the cops. They'll find you a safe place and even give you protection."

"Thank you, Boo. But how do I know I can trust you?"

"That didn't seem to worry you when you picked me up at the Coliseum. I helped you then, and I can help you now."

Vera looked around as if she thought some other guardian angel might appear.

"Vera. If I can find you, they can find you."

28

The highway was not well traveled in the evening, and the drive back down from Toulouse College was uneventful. We didn't talk much. Vera mostly slept. I envied her lack of paranoia. The radio kept me company. For most of the trip, I was able to pick up a folk music station that let me imagine I was riding the rails, leaving someone I loved, promising to come back when spring arrived, all the while strumming a guitar. We stopped for a snack at a rest stop on the side of the highway. I've forgotten what we ate—two murders and The Four Star Motel had crowded out any other thoughts. By the time we crossed the state line, the sun had set, a storm was brewing, and flashes of lightning lit the horizon. A few drops spattered on the windshield. When when we drove up to The Four Star Motel, the rain had become a steady drizzle, and the lightning promised something more dramatic. The office in front had large windows on two sides, and I could see the clerk sitting behind the desk. The attached cafeteria was deserted, except for a couple sitting at the counter. I'd seen that scene, a lonely café at night, in an Edward Hopper painting. Around back was the standard motel, two stories with rooms that opened onto parking places in front, and another set of doors that opened onto a balcony that ran the length of the building. Vera pointed to a spot in front of her room.

"I'll wait here, but please make it quick," I suggested. "This place gives me the creeps."

Vera walked to her door, fumbled with a key for a moment, and then disappeared inside. This place made me nervous. I had been a part of too much history here. Everything and everyone constantly watching and being watched. In my rearview mirror I could see a large two-cab pick-up with tinted windows parked at the end of the building. I'm sure I saw two thugs seated inside. A small sedan pulled up on the other side of the lot. Strange place to stop—it was not in front of any room. The woman in the driver's seat wore large dark glasses, and I think she kept checking me out. Sunglasses on a dark rainy night? And she was calling someone on her phone. Just then the couple left the restaurant and came out the back door of the motel office. They walked right toward me, faces covered with umbrellas held low against the rain. I pressed the lock on the doors and tried to look unconcerned. They came right up to the car, then walked around the back and into the room next to Vera's. And I could swear that the curtain in the room above Vera's moved to the side. Why was she taking so long? I was about to go check when the door opened and Vera appeared, dragging a suitcase. I unlocked the doors and helped her load the case into the back seat.

"Let's go," I pleaded.

"Be back in a minute, got to check out." Vera said cheerfully. She didn't seem to be aware of any of the looming threats that I had identified. I drove around front and kept an eye on her as she handed the key to the clerk. He watched her carefully as she came back to the car, then came to the window as we drove away. He was scratching his head, or maybe he was holding a cell phone to his ear.

Back on the road. Visibility was poor as we made our way along Lincoln Avenue. As we neared South Station, Vera suddenly said. "Boo, wait!"

"You can get your car tomorrow. Let's get out of this storm."

"I don't need my car. I have to go by the Factory. I have to find something."

I pulled over to the sidewalk. "The letter?"

"Yes. You know about it."

"You said they, whoever they were, were after it."

"So you took it?" Vera was getting upset.

"Yes."

"Do you still have it?" she asked hopefully.

"Well, not exactly." I hedged.

Vera looked at me with disbelief, as though she had just been betrayed. "Oh no! You gave it to Louella, didn't you?'

I nodded. Vera groaned. "Why?"

"Mr. Lafonte did set himself up by getting involved in an affair." I defended my actions, which were looking less and less defendable. "Do you know who Sweetie is?"

"No." Vera looked devastated. "But that letter can ruin Larry."

"Is that why you asked me to keep quiet—to protect Larry?"

"Yes. I wanted to destroy that damn letter."

"But wasn't that what you threatened him with, on the way to the station that night?"

"Yes, but no." Vera stammered. "I found that letter on the floor of the limo. We had a fight and I threatened to show it, that's all. I really wouldn't have used it."

"You had a fight with Larry in the limo, why? What about?"

"He said he was going to buy the Factory, and I would have to move out."

"Doesn't sound like the Mr. Lafonte I've met," I said.

"He said he didn't have any choice."

She didn't look at me, but stared out the front window. "I didn't really realize what could happen if that letter got into the wrong hands. I just put it in my purse after I found it. But when Larry said he had to throw me out, that he had no choice, I got angry and said if he did I'd . . . I don't know exactly what I said, just something about the letter."

"After the fight with Larry, you picked me up at the Coliseum Bar. Why?"

"Larry kinda lost it. Said I had to give him the letter. I was afraid he'd send someone after it. That factory is a lonely place. I saw you and . . . What were you doing in the bar anyway?"

"I was following you."

"You were following me? Why?"

"I was hoping to find out who Larry was having an affair with. You were a prime candidate. He even stayed at your place in the city."

"Oh, no! Larry and my father were lifelong friends. He was my godfather. Yes, he could sleep at my place if he wanted to. He'd come down to meet with his taxman and sometimes stayed over. So Lulu thinks I'm sleeping with her husband? That's crazy!"

We were parked by the side of the road across from South Station. I watched the late commuters drive out of the parking lot. I had to tell Vera about Louella.

"Have you talked with Larry recently?"

"Yes. A couple of days ago. I realized he would never send a guy with a gun after me. I called and told him I was sorry and never would have used the letter. He believed me, and we made up. He's been like a father to me, ever since my father died. He gave me the job at KittyLuv and everything."

"Vera, I don't think the contents of the letter are going to come out."

"Why?"

"You didn't see yesterday's papers. I'm sorry to tell you, but Louella was murdered."

Vera said nothing. She stared at me in confusion, as if searching her mind for a place that would accept the news of another murder. I took a deep breath and slowly recounted the details, trying unsuccessfully to lighten the news.

After a long silence Vera said, "I have to see Larry. How is he?"

I assured her that he was holding up okay, even though I really didn't know.

"I hope so," Vera said almost inaudibly. There was nothing left to say, and Vera curled up against the passenger door and closed her eyes. I pulled out into the driving rain.

29

I drove slowly along Lincoln Drive. Vera wasn't asleep; she just didn't want to open her eyes to the world. The rain was coming down in sheets. A bolt of lightning would display, for an instant, a wall of trees in a colorless palate, leaving a negative image of the scene to linger in my brain. Strong gusts of wind blew the Beamer from side to side. I wanted to get to the comfort of the Arms, where we could hide behind a martini and watch the storm rant and rave harmlessly over the rail yards.

Visibility was only about fifty feet, and the guy behind me was driving with his high beams on. I turned onto Machinist's Drive; it was deserted except for the high-beamer, who had also turned. He started to pass. He obviously didn't know the road, as we were approaching the one-lane bridge over Hammer Creek. I slowed to let him go by. It was the doublecab pick-up truck that I recognized from the motel parking lot, and it pulled alongside me. The passenger window was only feet away, it was open, and the barrel of a pistol poked out, aimed directly at my face. Knockout's grinning mug was behind it. I hit the brakes at the same moment he fired. The bullet hit my windshield; the safety glass held the thousand small bits in place, creating a glistening opaque screen. I couldn't see a thing in front of us. The truck swerved and smashed into my door, the air bag exploded into my chest. Now the Beamer was following his instructions and not mine, and his instructions were to send us over the edge of the road, twenty-five feet down the vertical drop into Hammer Creek. Vera screamed as we skidded over the edge. We spun over, hit the ground, and spun over again. Up wasn't up any more. It only took a few seconds—my life didn't flash before me; I was busy wondering if my insurance would cover a double flip into the rocks below. With a deafening crash of shredding metal and exploding glass we came to a stop, upside down. Vera and I were hanging by our seatbelts. Water was running through my broken window, over the top of my head, and out the other side. The Beamer was lying on its roof, halfway into the stream. Vera had stopped screaming, a trickle of blood ran down her cheek. She was struggling to get out of her seat belt.

I heard a sharp crack and a thud shook the car. I looked through what used to be my car window and saw an upside-down figure standing at the edge of the road above, aiming his pistol down at us. Another shot. Knockout was firing at us. I knew the gas tank was a good target, but we were in a pitch-black gulley. Knockout was lit from behind by the lights of the two-cab—a perfect target if I was right side up. I managed to pull my Glock from the holster, hung upside down from the belt and aimed, both hands steadying the grip. KO fired again, and I fired. The black shape stood motionless on the side of the road above, then slowly pivoted forward and fell, bouncing crazily down the rocks, growing larger and larger, until it crashed against the side of the Beamer, covering my shattered window. Then it slid down and lay in a motionless heap in a half-foot of water by the top of the car. I fired at the cab of the truck that showed over the edge. I hit something, but the truck jerked forward and sprayed gravel down the slope. I could see its taillights shrinking away on the other side of the bridge. No sign of life from the dark hulk that used to be Knockout. He was either dead or ninety percent dead.

Vera had quit struggling, and was staring at me, and trying to hold her dress down. I braced myself with one hand and reached over with the other to pull her hair away from her face. The blood was coming from a scratch that didn't appear serious. The only reassuring thing I could think of to say was, "Just stick with me and you'll be safe." Realizing how dumb that was, I tried again. "Are you okay?"

Vera choked out a "Yes, I think so," and started to cry. I had been hoping she wouldn't cry so I could, but one of us had to untangle this mess. I'd never practiced getting out of a seatbelt upside down, and it turned out to be rather difficult. But the truck was gone, Knockout was no longer a threat, and we were only about a foot into the creek, so there was no reason to panic. We managed to free ourselves from the straps, and lay in a crumpled mass on the inside of the roof of the car. The doors were crushed and wouldn't open, and I felt a nasty pain working its way up my left arm. The jagged glass edges in the window prevented us from crawling out. I started kicking on the door as hard as I could, trying to force it open. I stopped and glanced over at Vera. She had gotten herself together and was holding her cell phone. "Where are we?" she asked.

I told her and she relayed it all to the dispatcher on the line. I was about to start kicking the door again when Vera reached over and took my arm. "Boo. We're okay, I think. So let's get comfortable. They shouldn't be too long."

I looked at Vera. She was the most beautiful person in the world. I reached out and took her in my arms, or just my right arm, for the left one was not working. Outside the rain poured down, the wind rocked the trees above, and water from the creek seeped into our clothes. We folded together like a couple of wet kittens and waited for someone to come and take us home.

30

Last night, Vera and I gave brief statements to the police while we waited to be treated at the hospital. A nurse tended to the scrape on Vera's forehead while Dr. Sanji pulled a puddle of glass pieces out of my arm. If one wanted to write a mystery and needed a plot line, just spend some time in the emergency ward at two in the morning. A married couple with both their heads bandaged sat across from us. From their argument, it was not clear which one had hit the other on the head with a hammer, or who was supposed to water the plants when they got home. A young guy was there with his parents. Half the contents of their medical cabinet had just been pumped out of his stomach, and they were waiting for the results of some test. A gurney was pushed through the room, and I couldn't determine whether the body lying on it was dead or alive. By then I had completely forgotten about the shards of glass that were lodged in my left arm.

I clearly remembered the arm a half hour later when Dr. Sanji was pulling the glass pieces out. She was kind and gentle, but it still hurt like hell. I tried to focus on Dr. Sanji. How did a young woman with a lovely British accent end up at the New Memorial Hospital? I imagined her in a sari. I was slowly turning her around, unwrapping the soft fabric that circled her body. I remembered an illustration from the Kama Sutra, and as she turned I was recreating the naked image. But each time I was about to pull the last wisp of fabric aside Dr. Sanji pulled another piece of glass from my arm and the sari wrapped itself closed like a window blind. Unwinding the brightly colored silk sari again—her body slowly revealing itself—another turn, another piece of glass dug out of my arm, and I had to start over again. Fortunately, Dr. Sanji was a fine seamstress, and she expertly sewed my arm back together.

It was five in the morning before we were told to go sleep it off and come back to the police station tomorrow afternoon. Vera left to stay at Kathy's, and a squad car drove me back to the Arms. I needed a martini. I had heard that the hardest part of wearing a sling was getting dressed, but they totally under-estimated the difficulty in getting the ice out of an ice cube tray. There wasn't much of the night left for sleeping—I used the martini as a sedative and dozed fitfully in my armchair.

. . . .

Inspector Corbutt came by The Arms around noon to pick me up and drive me to the station. Young Tom the recruit was in the front seat with Corbutt. They put me in back. I convinced Corbutt to stop at the bridge over Hammer Creek so I could look down at the twisted wreckage of my deceased Beamer. It was lying on its side at the edge of the creek. Last night the emergency crew had to roll it over onto its side with us in it in order to use the jaws of death to pry the door off. They had set up bright spotlights to shine down from above, and when they rolled the car it brought back the terror we felt when we were spinning out of control down the slope. We were helped out of the car, up the incline, and wrapped in blankets in the back of an ambulance.

Corbutt, Tom, and I left the Hammer Creek view. Cor-butt's next stop was South Station. Vera had given me the keys so that I could pick up her car. Corbutt dropped me off and waited until I found Vera's white Ford Focus. Then the black-and-white police car turned onto the Avenue and I watched it until South Station blocked the view. Suddenly I felt very much alone. I started up the Ford and was about to drive out of the lot when I spotted a familiar, large, black, two-cab pick-up truck. I instinctively grabbed for my pistol, only to remem-ber that the police had confiscated it. I parked Vera's car, got out, and carefully approached the truck. I was relieved that no one was inside. The right side was badly scraped, and I recognized a streak of rust that belonged to my ex-Beamer. The window on the passenger side was shattered. There was a small hole in the frame above the door. I was sure that a search of the cab would turn up a shell or two that matched my Glock. I punched JJ's number into my cell and let him know what I had found, then stayed away from the guilty ve-hicle in the off chance that someone would come to reclaim it.

It didn't take long for a blinking squad car to arrive. The passenger door opened and JJ stepped out. "Blue. I heard you had quite a night. How's the arm?"

"It's okay. Just a scratch." I pointed to the truck. "Look what I found."

"Is this the one?" JJ asked. I nodded. JJ tried the door. It was open. A quick search of the glove compartment and he was holding the registration and insurance card. "A company in the city. Let me check this out." He took the registration back to the police car.

I looked inside. There was nothing unusual. Some carpen-try tools on the floor of the back seat, a few pieces of leftover lumber in the bed.

JJ returned. "Stolen." He announced. "Yesterday morning. Taken off the street in Brooklyn. Your attackers intended to do something nasty and wanted an unmarked vehicle to cover their tracks."

"And a big heavy one to boot," I said. "One large enough to push a poor unsuspecting Beamer off a cliff." I was mourning the loss of my car, even though it was so old and run down it was about to die a natural death. "They stole this machine in Brooklyn, drove it up here, used it, then parked it here and took the train back to the city. Or I should say, one of them took the train back."

I waited in Vera's Ford while JJ filed his report, then followed him back to the center of town and parked in the lot behind LeRoy's. The storm was over, the town was washed clean, and the sun was trying to dissolve the remaining clouds. The events of last night were slowly sinking in. I didn't like to shoot people, even rotters like Knockout. It left me with too many "what if" scenarios. As I walked along the edge of the Park to the police headquarters, I reworked the events in my mind. Could I have avoided that confrontation? If I wasn't so paranoid at The Four Stars Motel, I might have picked out the real threat from all the others that I had imagined. But paranoia has served me well in the past, and I wasn't about to look for a cure.

Vera was waiting at the police station when I arrived. She was fine. She had a scratch on her forehead and wore the band-aid as though it were a status symbol. She was dressed for the interview in a short skirt, low-cut haltertop, and light jacket. Her heels were a good two inches higher than those she normally wore. The sudden interest in her had left Vera feeling like a celebrity, and she wanted to dress the part.

I was ushered to the interrogation suite and waited outside while they talked with Vera. As she left the room, she smiled at me and followed Tom the recruit down the hall. I was called in. I didn't like the room, and I didn't like the self-important guy who was assigned to grill me, but I had killed someone and the police had to follow procedure. I told him about finding Vera at Toulouse, driving her back, stopping by The Four Star Motel, and the drama at Hammer Creek. I told him when and where I'd run into Knockout and who he was and where he worked. I filled him in on Vera's relationship with Lawrence Lafonte. My Beamer was full of bullet holes. I was sure that some lead would be found and matched to Knockout's pistol. Also, Vera could back up my story. Nevertheless, the examiner acted as if everything I said was new to him. It didn't matter that Vera had told him the same thing a half hour earlier. The official interview ended. Kathy and JJ were waiting in the next room where they had watched the proceedings through the one-way glass. Kathy told us to go to her office; she'd be along in a few minutes. I was relieved to be free of the inquisition and looking forward to talking with Kathy and JJ.

The Chief's new right-hand man, Georgio, was at his desk when I arrived at Kathy's office. He was a new acquisition; I'd only met him once before. He was much too good-looking to be Kathy's assistant; he should have been featured as August in the policeman's calendar.

I introduced myself. "Hi. Name's Blue."

"Glad to meet you, Blue. I'm Georgio." He didn't remember me. "I'm sure Chief MacGregor will be back in a minute."

"By the way, Georgio. Do you need a job?"

Georgio looked at me, puzzled. "I already have a job."

"Hmmm. I thought so."

Fortunately, Kathy arrived.

After a slow day at the sterile police station, Kathy's office was warm and downright cozy. The sun had beaten the clouds and was hovering in the western sky. The office windows looked over the Park, and I watched the shadows of the build- ings stretch across the grass to touch Number Six's bench. He had left early today.

Kathy tenderly touched my left arm. "Blue, how are you feeling?"

"Not too good until now. You just cheered me up."

JJ shifted in his seat and coughed. I think he didn't want to sit through any teenage banter between his Chief and his good friend.

"What's happening with Vera?" I asked.

"She'll be staying at my place for a couple of days." Kathy left my side and took her seat behind the Chief's desk. "She is remarkably cool about the whole thing. Seems to think she's starring in a popular TV series. Takes to the part like a mati- nee idol."

"She'll be protected?" I was concerned.

"For the present. I've arranged for a twenty-four hour po- lice watch." Kathy explained. "We'll see what happens next. I suspect that you took care of the biggest threat."

"Yeah. Knockout. Sorry to see him go."

JJ stepped in. "Yes, Knockout. His prints suggest that his mother called him Paolo Calibano."

"Makes him sound almost human," I murmured to myself.

JJ went on, "He's been in and out of the clink for much of his life. Accused of murder a few year ago, but got off."

Kathy asked, "What case was that?"

"A Dimitri Topolis was found strangled in his bathtub in his town house on New York City's Upper East Side."

"He was the head of Topolis Industries. Weren't they a big real estate firm?" Kathy remembered the case.

That made sense to me. "It would be interesting to see how Sidney Jones and Diamond Realty profited from that convenient death."

Kathy sat back and looked at me. "You've been pretty clear about all the events, but I'd like to hear some of your theories. Why were they trying to kill Vera, or you?"

"They were really after Vera, although I'm sure that Knockout, or Calibano as you call him, wouldn't have lost much sleep if he bumped me off at the same time."

"Go on." Kathy and JJ prepared to hear me out.

"It was beginning to look like Lafonte would cave to Jones's demands."

"Which were . . . ? Kathy asked.

"Lafonte controls an option to buy the Factory. It was given to him years ago by Vera's father—he borrowed money from Lafonte and used the option as collateral. I think Jones has something on Lafonte, and was pressuring him to buy the place and resell it to Diamond Realty."

"How does Vera fit in?" JJ asked.

"Vera wanted to prevent Diamond Realty from tearing down her Factory and building the massive Hope Estates upper-crust housing development, but she couldn't prevent the sale if Lafonte wanted to go ahead. She was working on a back-up plan. One way to sabotage their plans was to find lead on the site. Wouldn't even matter how much, just the hint of lead pollution would rob Sidney Jones of millions of dollars."

"Wouldn't that also kill the museum idea?" JJ asked.

"I don't think so. Vera knows a lot about lead; after all, her father ran a pipe factory. They quit making lead pipes early in the century, and lead doesn't tend to seep far into the soil. The building is stone, the floors concrete and slate, and there's no lead paint in the place. Chances are if she could get rid of the stacks of junk and take six inches of earth off the surface, the place would be fine. Nobody is going to get lead poisoning visiting the museum. In theory Diamond Realty could also do that, but they want to sell million-dollar mansions. They could get rid of the lead, but they'd never get rid of the stigma."

"So she finds a guy to test for lead," JJ adds.

"Exactly. She runs into Jim Alexander when she's up at Toulouse with Lafonte for a fundraiser. Hires him to come down and get some samples from the soil. She meets him in the Coliseum Bar and sends him to an old drainage ditch. If there were any lead around, it would be there. But somebody, probably Sidney Jones, has been told that Alexander was coming. He sends his hit man. I saw Knockout that night at the bar. He killed Alexander, strangled him, and put him on the tracks where he'd lose his head. That was supposed to scare off Vera and get her to give up the fight."

"How did Jones know Alexander would be at the Coliseum Bar?" Kathy asked. "Who's been tipping him off? And," Kathy began to list the unknowns, "who else was in the truck that ran you off the road last night? And what do they have on Lafonte that can force his hand?"

"And," JJ added, "who killed Louella Lafonte?"

"And," JJ and Kathy said in unison, "who is Sweetie?"

"She must be wearing the Helmet of Hades," I said to no one in particular.

"The what?" JJ frowned.

"Put it on and it makes you invisible. Hades, the Lord of the Underworld, had it, but people, or gods, kept borrowing it. He lent it to Perseus to help him in his battle with Medusa. Probably wouldn't have worked, though; it was her look that turned people to stone. He chopped off her head while she was reflected in his shield. But he used the helmet to get away from her sisters—they were Gorgons, you know. Not very nice."

JJ and Kathy waited politely for me to finish.

"Sweetie must be wearing the helmet. She's right in the middle of us, but remains invisible."

JJ suddenly remembered an important appointment and excused himself.

Kathy and I looked at each other. She drummed her desk with her bright red nails. "Blue, I had enough trouble convincing the DA not to charge you with something. So if you could try to stay out of a trouble for a couple of days . . ." She paused. "I know it will be hard, but if you could . . ."

"I'll give it a shot."

"A shot?" Kathy repeated skeptically.

"How about dinner. A cocktail at LeRoy's, and then we could go over to Sammy's Steakhouse." I think my sling was softening Kathy's heart.

"It's a date, Blue. How about Monday, I've got the day off."

"What about your friend, with a job?"

"That's the problem," Kathy sighed. "The fucking job."

"The fucking job?"

"Yes. All he talks about is his fucking job. Boring as hell."

"You wouldn't have that problem with me."

"That's for sure," Kathy said. "Monday then." Kathy smiled one of those smiles that would reappear in my dreams.

31

Buy-Right Auto Insurance had offered me the blue book value of my BMW coupe, minus the five hundred dollar deductible. I'll have to check with Rick Jones Used Cars to see what I can get for about three hundred dollars. Maybe I can buy my old Honda back. The insurance company did offer to pay for a rental for five days while my car was being repaired. Repaired? Not much chance, but I took them up on the offer and rented a spiffy silver four-door sedan, all shiny and clean and reeking of new car smell. It looked like a large sneaker. It beeped and flashed its blinkers as I approached with the key. It put my seatbelt on for me when I closed the door. The array of lights behind the steering wheel flashed to warn me to do something, and a soothing female voice told me I should release the brake. I wasn't sure whether I was driving the car or it was letting me come along for the ride. There were buttons for gears, which came in handy, as I was a one-arm driver. The engine didn't make a sound, and I think I dozed off on the way into town to meet Doctor Dollar, but my new lady friend reminded me to stay awake.

I turned into the driveway that sloped down beside Le-Roy's and parked in the lot in back. I was about to walk back up and around to the front when Joey, LeRoy's clean-up guy, came out of the back door with five bursting bags of garbage. The strip club was on the level below the bar, and its back door opened onto the parking lot. One normally entered the club through the street door of the bar, paid a fee, and went downstairs to watch the action. Patrons could leave the club through the back door, with, or without, an escort. The dancing often continued inside the parked cars.

Joey dropped the garbage bags by the drive and went back inside, leaving the door open, so I could take a short cut through the club, up the stairs, and into the bar.

The strip club was deserted; the chairs turned upside down on top of the tables to allow Joey to mop the floor. One could only imagine the flashing red lights that circled the stage, the heavy musical rhythm, the crowd of boisterous drinkers waiting for the strippers to wrap themselves around the poles. In the daylight the room looked like a school cafeteria after the kids had gone home. The four brass poles, unable to go home with anyone, were left to watch over the empty room.

I stood at the bottom of the stairs and looked over the club. The overhead lights dimmed, the red stage lights came on and began to rotate, sending beams about the room. The large speakers throbbed with a steady beat. Stella Starlight appeared on stage and the crowd shouted approval. She was sporting six-inch heels, a brassiere that carried more jewels than Miss America's tiara, and a mini skirt made up of shimmering strips of fabric that did a lousy job of hiding a nearly nonexistent g-string. Stella grabbed a pole and wrapped one leg around it. She looked across the crowd directly at me, reached around her back with one hand, unsnapped the glittering top, and tossed it onto a table of hypnotized lawyers. Her breasts, excited by their freedom, swung left and right searching the room for lustful eyes. Stella twisted and writhed on the pole, slowly transforming herself into an overall-clad chunky guy. Joey was polishing the poles. He held a pole with one hand and with the other slid an oil-stained cloth up and down the brass. The metal glistened, even in the dull interior light. I took the stairs to the bar.

LeRoy was sliding an oil-stained cloth across the mahogany bar. Doctor Dollar hadn't arrived. It was too early for a martini, but not for a beer. I took my stool at the far end of the bar. LeRoy looked at the sling.

"You know you made the papers this morning."

I didn't know, so LeRoy found a copy of the *The Journal* under the bar and laid it and a draft beer in front of me. It was lunchtime, so he added a bowl of pretzels.

The headline read: 'SECURITY GUARD SHOT—COUPLE DRIVES OFF BRIDGE.'

I looked at LeRoy. "I didn't exactly drive off."

"I figured that. What happened?" LeRoy wanted a juicy tidbit that he could tell his customers that evening.

"Some guy from the city—you know how they drive— wanted my lane. So he took it." The rest of the article didn't clear anything up. The reporter was struggling to piece together a story. I discovered that the security guard stood in the road to try to warn us about something and I swerved to avoid him and he shot himself by accident as he jumped out of the way. Some guy who worked at The Four Star Motel recognized what was left of my car, and said he'd seen a couple that looked like Vera and me coming out of one of the rooms earlier that evening. When fame comes your way it's never the fame you dreamed of.

"Good day." Henry Cadman was standing beside me.

I pushed the paper away. "Doctor. How are you? Thanks for coming by. Let's sit over there." I motioned toward a nearby table. "LeRoy. Bring the good Doctor a beer."

He waved off the beer. "Too early. My work day is just starting." We shifted to the table. "Is it broken?" The Doctor asked about my arm.

"No. Just a scratch. And I don't use this arm much anyway."

"If I were you, I would have run the guy over instead of driving off the cliff."

"Yeah. Bad decision," I agreed. "And if I were the guard I wouldn't have shot myself with the gun of the guy I just ran off the road."

LeRoy heard that. Now he had a good story for the evening crowd. The Doctor laughed and let it go. "I have some stuff for you, about KittyLuv's finances."

"Shoot," I said.

"Probably shouldn't say that," LeRoy called from the bar.

"Benny's been looking around," the Doctor went on. "And when Benny starts looking you can forget about Internet privacy."

"He'd never get me. I'm password protected."

"You don't have a pet, so your password is your birthday. Right?"

"Right."

The Doctor opened his attaché case, placed a folder on the table, and patted it. "In here are copies of KittyLuv's tax returns, and some forms they file to maintain a tax-exempt status. It's hard to sort out, as the accounting is pretty sophisticated."

"You see something funny, don't you?" I asked. Doctor Dollar was about to tell me the reason for Thalia's use of the word "but."

"They take in quite a bit from all over the place. It's hard to account for it all. To their credit, the administrative costs are not a big percentage of the operation. The curious thing is that a chunk of money, a couple of hundred thou, seems to have been lent out."

"Loans? KittyLuv is not in the banking business."

"Exactly, so it's a bit odd. Problem is there's no requirement to say who the borrower is. I can't find the terms or see any interest coming in."

"An inside job, maybe," I was showing off my sophisticated financial knowledge.

"No doubt. It's not uncommon; the banks give loans to their execs all the time, and with good terms. But it's strange for KittyLuv, although it's probably legal."

"Even if it's legal it would be tough on their reputation if it came out. Money's supposed to go to kittens." I began to wonder about KittyLuv. " Did you find anything else?"

"Aside from that one big chunk of money, everything else balances out. It looks legit to me." The Doctor replaced the folder and closed his case.

"Thanks, Doctor. You've been very helpful, as you always are. Don't worry, I'll get the tab."

"I didn't have anything." He stood up to leave. "By the way, Blue, any chance you could bring me some financial info one of these days?"

"On what? What do I know about high finance?"

"High finance, my ass!" He laughed. "I was thinking of your tax returns. April fifteenth was four months ago."

"C'mon, Doctor, it's August. Everyone knows the IRS takes the summer off."

Henry Cadman left, and I returned to the stool at the end of the bar. I needed another beer before I could tackle Larry Lafonte.

LeRoy brought a beer over. He slid a bowl of peanuts and another of cheese chips in front of me. "You know, your friends were in here last night."

"Who's that?"

"The chauffeur guy, and three of the gals who work at KittyLuv."

"Which ones? Did you recognize them?"

"Let's see. There was a thin wispy girl, reddish hair with a silver streak. She kinda floats about."

"Sounds like Sybil Troy, Lafonte's secretary."

"And a shorter, round one. Nice face, short black hair, and a twinkle in her eye."

"Rose, I'll bet."

"And a thin tall girl, with a long face. She looked young enough to prompt me to check her driver's license."

"Don't know who that would be, maybe Betty."

"Let me check the bar tabs." LeRoy took a pile of receipts from under the bar and leafed through them. "Here, the bar tabs." He smoothed two slips of paper out on the bar and turned them toward me.

Samson had signed one, and the other was difficult to read, but it looked like Rose Christensen. "How come her bill is triple Samson's?"

"He only pays for himself. She covered the drinks for the three women. I think they chipped in."

"Doesn't look like a way to get on the good side of the ladies. How did the evening go?"

"The usual. Samson gets a bit drunk and starts to get rowdy. The gals left, and I encouraged him to follow."

I looked at the tabs again. "LeRoy, I'll be dammed!"

"What?"

"You've just told me who Sweetie is!"

"Sweetie?" LeRoy scratched his head. "Sounds like you've identified half of my customers."

32

Sybil was not her wispy self. Rose was at her desk but wouldn't look at me. The mood in the office was somber. Sybil wanted to ask me who the hell I was and what was I after, but she just motioned toward a chair. Her boss's wife was dead. The office was in a state of shock. Lafonte was a walking ghost. He was coming to work because he didn't know what else to do, and the Doolittle guy had just raged at her about nothing. The last couple of weeks had rattled the quiet nature of our town. A man's beheaded body was found on the tracks near Vera's factory. Then the wife of one of the most respected citizens was brutally murdered. Vera shows up in an upside-down wreck in Hammer Creek. A dead man is lying beside the car. Vera was in that car with a mysterious detective, the very same guy who brought a cat to the office last week and who is now sitting quietly in the corner waiting to see Mr. Lafonte.

I tried unsuccessfully to lighten the mood with some talk about the weather, but neither Rose nor Sybil looked my way. The intercom buzzed, and Sybil pointed toward Lafonte's office without looking at me. I found Lafonte sitting motionless, sunk into his soft chair beside his desk. He didn't jump up and greet me with that fundraiser enthusiasm. The normally bright eyes were dull and watery, the smile had vanished, the mustache looked wilted, and his hair seemed to have become grayer. Unread reports were scattered aimlessly about his desk, and a few sheets of paper lay forgotten on the floor. He looked at me with the eyes of a plaster statue.

"Mr. Lafonte. I want to say, about Louella, it is an unbelievable tragedy. I don't know exactly how I fit in, but I feel that the letter had something to do with it. I'd just like to say I'm sorry. I may have . . ."

Lafonte interrupted. "The marriage was over. There's nothing that could save it. Lulu knew that I was in the midst of an affair, and she would have followed up on it one way or another." Lafonte rubbed his eyes. "But who would have killed her?"

"Maybe it was a random tragedy. Some thief who was caught in the act."

Lafonte just shook his head.

"Can you talk for a moment?"

He shrugged. "Certainly. What else can go wrong?"

"One good piece of news. Vera is doing well. She got a small scratch in the accident. The police are keeping her in a safe place."

Lafonte nodded. "Poor child. She doesn't deserve any of this."

"The guy who tried to bump her off, who got shot . . ."

Lafonte interrupted. "Who you shot, I'm told."

"Yes, that's true. He worked for Diamond Realty. Somebody there is willing to go to any length to get the Bishop Factory land."

"Tell me about it," Lafonte said with a sarcastic upturn of his mustache.

"If they can't force you to close on the option, maybe they could force Vera to sell. And if that doesn't work, just get her out of the picture and buy it from her estate lawyers. Why did they think that they could force you to buy the place and turn it over to them?"

Lafonte was silent.

"What does Marcus Doolittle have on you?"

More silence.

"He's a dead beat, a loafer, and part-time crook. Yet you gave him a raise and a promotion. Doolittle found some problem in the finances of this place, didn't he?"

"What does it matter?" Lafonte slowly spread his hands, palms up to the heavens.

"What about the couple of hundred thousand not accounted for?"

I expected Lafonte to react, but his expression didn't change. I waited for him to explain.

"Yes, there's money unaccounted for, but I didn't steal anything—it's a loan. I just borrowed a bunch; it's not illegal."

"Not illegal," I agreed. "But enough to bring KittyLuv to its knees if it made the papers. If that story came out funds would disappear faster than cat food from an animal shelter."

"You're right." Lafonte had lost the will to fight. "Donors need to trust the organization absolutely."

"Is Doolittle blackmailing you?"

Lafonte just looked at me. I think it was his version of taking the fifth.

"Can you pay it back?"

"Not unless I sell the house, but now I guess I can do that."

I wasn't sure I should, but I tried a different tack. "I think your chauffeur is a bit of a loose cannon. What are the chances he could be mixed up in this somehow?"

"Samson? No way. He's the most loyal guy on my staff."

"He's the guy who chased Vera through the Factory with a loaded gun the last time he overheard something."

"I still can't believe that!" Lafonte said angrily. "Vera thought I sent him after her—that's nonsense."

I was facing a broken man. Lafonte was in the middle of two murders, but he's a well-meaning guy who wanted to help kittens. He seemed trapped between one side of his personality where he was playing with fire—a shady loan and a hidden affair—and on the other side, a generous guy who would bend over backwards to help his goddaughter, Vera. If you have two sides to your personality, at some point they're going to meet, and they probably won't get along.

"I'm sorry, Mr. Lafonte. I'll leave you alone."

"Are you going to the press with all this stuff, the loan, the letter, and who knows what they'll come up with next?"

"No. I'm a detective, not a reporter." I put out my hand. Lafonte took it reluctantly. The strong handshake was gone.

He stared after me as I left the room. Sybil and Rose watched silently as I let myself out. I doubted I would ever return to the KittyLuv offices. I was wrong.

33

Kathy had taken the day off and taken her uniform off as well. She met me in the evening outside the Police Headquarters wearing a light sundress that matched the August heat. Her shoulders were bare and bronze. The top two buttons of the dress were undone, which made me want to visit the nude beach where she got her tan. Open-toed sandals showed off bright red nail polish that matched her long fingernails. Her only features that maintained a modicum of modesty were her blue eyes, which were hiding behind large dark sunglasses.

We met at the edge of the Park and walked over to Le-Roy's. We planned to enjoy a cocktail before walking down the block to Sammy's Steakhouse for a nice dinner. I convinced Kathy to join me for a dry martini.

She toasted me and asked, "So what's it like rolling off a cliff with a cute little redhead?"

"It's a good way to get to know someone. But making love hanging upside down halfway into a stream while being shot at is not easy."

Kathy smiled and had a suggestion. "We could go by the playground later and practice on the jungle gym."

"How's Vera doing?" I asked.

"She's fine, but she is not anxious to go back to work. Her boss, what's-his-name, has soured the financial office."

"Marcus Doolittle."

"Yes, him. What is he up to?"

"I'm sure I could get it out of him if I got the chance."

Kathy looked across the bar. "Speaking of the devil, look over there."

Marcus Doolittle was sitting at the far end of the bar. He was staring into an empty glass. This was too tempting to miss.

"What do you say, Kathy, let's try a little role play here. We need to scare him, see if we can get him to admit to something. I'm going over to buy him a drink. Maybe I can warm him up."

"Not if you're a private eye, you won't. Especially if you've been sitting with the Chief of Police."

"True. But he's never met me. The only time our paths crossed he was sleeping in front of his computer. I doubt he knows you, and in that dress you certainly don't look like the Chief of Police. Why don't you go tart yourself up a bit, and I'll go over and sell your services."

"You want me to be a prostitute?"

"It's a time-tested way to affect a man's good judgment. And it wouldn't be so hard, would it? You've got the looks, and the body. All you need is a little attitude adjustment."

"Do I have to fuck him?"

"Probably not. Maybe just a caress or two." I was afraid Kathy rather liked the idea.

"Okay. But with one provision."

"What's that?"

"After this is over, I get to sleep with the pimp." Kathy smiled at me.

"I could probably arrange that." Kathy left for the ladies room. I walked over to the bar and sat down next to Marcus and started the conversation. "Mind if I buy you a drink?"

Doolittle looked up from his empty glass. "Who the hell are you?"

"Just a businessman. I can see you need some company. Thought I could help."

"Not your kind of company," he growled.

"No, you're right. But I have a friend. I'm sure she could cheer you up."

Marcus showed some interest. "Who?"

I tipped my head toward the table. Kathy had returned. She'd undone another button on her dress. He legs were crossed to display a long length of bare thigh. She was staring at her nails as if they were the most interesting things that ever crossed her mind.

Marcus stared at her. "That one?"

I motioned Kathy to come over. LeRoy watched from the other end of the bar. I pointed to Marcus's empty glass. Kathy slid onto the stool on the other side of Marcus. She leaned forward, and I thought her breasts were going to bounce out and rest on the mahogany bar.

"What's your name, big fella?" Kathy asked, touching his arm.

"Ah," he hesitated, "Joe. Joe Smith," he stuttered.

LeRoy replaced Joe Smith's empty glass with a double shot and gave me a martini.

"Cheers," I raised my glass.

Joe raised his and drank. If he kept on like that, the alcohol and Kathy's boobs would replace any common sense he was trying to hold on to. He tried to stay in charge. "What happened to your arm?"

"Oh, just a little problem. Sometimes I do a little, let's just say, work on the side, if you know what I mean. It can be a risky business."

Kathy moved her knee against Joe's leg. He hesitated, then asked me, "Who hires you?"

"Oh it's always the New York crowd. You know, when they have money involved around here, I get work. They know they can rely on me. So, Joe, you going to hire this little lady? I can't wait. I've got to go over to . . . do you know where the place called KittyLuv is?"

"Why do you want to go there?' Joe was confused.

"Oh, I have to, let's say, talk with a guy there. It's just a job." I raised my glass again and encouraged Joe to do the same.

He was getting worried. "Who hired you?" The words came out in a bit of a jumble.

"A guy named Jones. Probably not his real name, who'd be named Jones these days. But what do I care. Money's money."

Joe was turning a lighter shade of pale. I'd warmed him up enough. Time to turn up the pressure "Look, Joe. I know your name is not Smith. You're Doolittle, the guy who got a nice promotion to be head of KittyLuv's accounting office."

"What? So?"

"You're hired as a low-level accountant. Then you prowl through the books and discover that Lafonte has loaned himself a chunk of money. You threaten to tell the papers that the head of KittyLuv is spending money on himself rather than cute kittens, and, guess what, you're suddenly promoted."

Kathy slid closer to Doolittle, rubbed her left hand over his balding head, and came to his defense. "Sounds to me like if there's anyone to blame it's, what's his name, Lafonte. He was doing the shady dealing." I couldn't see Kathy's right hand as it was under the bar, and I suspected it was playing with Doolittle's mind.

"Damn right." Doolittle was eager to agree. "I didn't take any money, and I deserve to be the head of accounting. Those girls didn't know what they were doing anyway."

"But what about the money from Jones?" I pressed him.

"What money? What did he tell you?" Doolittle's voice rose.

"You overheard Vera talking about Diamond Realty and Lafonte's option to buy and realized that you were sitting on a gold mine. So you contact Jones. He gets some dirt that he can use to pressure Lafonte, and you get dollars."

Kathy leaned closer. "You're quite the mover. And I can tell you're a pretty big guy. C'mon, Joe. We could have a lot of fun."

"Yes," Doolittle said, suddenly seeing a way out. "Let's go."

"But there is a question of money, you know," Kathy purred. "I have expensive tastes, and maybe you could share a bit of the profits with me."

Doolittle's brain had shifted down to between his legs. "I didn't get that much."

"But," I kept going. "What about the second payoff from DR? That must have been a doozy."

"What payoff? For what?"

"You talked with Jim Alexander at Toulose and learned he was coming down to check the land for lead contamination." At the very mention of Alexander's name Doolittle jerked enough to knock his glass over. It was nearly empty, and I motioned to LeRoy, who promptly brought a full one. "You see more dollars. You call Jones and tell him Alexander is coming down. Jones pays you for the info and sends Knockout to take care of Alexander."

"Who's Knockout?" It was all Doolittle could come up with.

"I guess you call him Calibano. But things got out of hand. Alexander is dead; his head chopped off on the railroad tracks after somebody, you, tipped off the murderer. Now you've become an accessory to murder. Probably not something you planned on."

Marcus panicked. "I didn't kill anybody, it was Calibano!"

"Sure, who's going to believe that?"

"I didn't know they'd kill him, really," Marcus pleaded.

"You just thought they'd rough him up a bit?"

"Yes, no. I mean, I thought they'd just keep him from getting the samples." He nervously pulled at his tie. I think the hair growing out of his ears turned white.

"Then Calibano was shot at Hammer Creek after somebody forced a car off the road." I looked him in the eye.

Marcus looked at my sling. "You?"

"Yep. Me. And I saw you driving that two-cab pickup, and you also left some prints in it. Marcus Doolittle, you are in big fucking trouble."

"I've been set up!" Marcus groaned.

"You helped Calibano try to kill me," I pressed.

"I didn't want to. Jones had me, said he'd turn me in if I didn't drive."

"And Louella Lafonte?"

Doolittle looked surprised. "Louella? No way. I had nothing to do with that. You have to believe me."

"Why would I believe you?"

"Really! I swear. I didn't have nothing to do with Louella."

"You've got one chance to survive this, to avoid a murder rap. The cops would rather go after the big guys."

"Jones?" Marcus asked, knowing the answer. Marcus gulped down the last of his drink. He treated it like the last drink he might have in a long while, and he didn't want to waste a drop. He had no good alternatives, and he knew it. "Who's going to believe *you?*" He desperately challenged.

"Well, Chief MacGregor for one," I said. Marcus followed my gaze toward Kathy. She had let go of his brain and was holding up her badge for him to see.

"Oh fuck, no!" Marcus looked around, desperate for a way out.

Kathy morphed into the policewoman. "Marcus Doolittle. You are under arrest for extortion and accessory to murder."

"How about reckless driving," I offered helpfully.

Kathy looked him in the eye. "Mr. Doolittle, you promise to testify and you can get a plea bargain. You're talking maybe five to ten instead of life without parole." She reached into her purse and came up with a pair of handcuffs.

Marcus stared at her. His hands shook so much I thought LeRoy was about to lose another glass. Doolittle would sing and keep singing, that was clear. This was a guy who would rat on his grandmother to avoid a parking ticket. He didn't resist when Kathy pulled his arms behind his back and snapped the lock. Kathy took out her cell phone and tapped a call button. Almost instantly the door to the bar opened and Corbutt and Thomas entered. Corbutt watched the perp closely; Tom watched Kathy's breasts closely.

The Chief gave the orders. "Take this guy, read him his rights, and book him."

"The charge?" Corbutt asked.

"For now, extortion." She looked at Doolittle. "We'll see what else later."

Corbutt and Tom efficiently marched Doolittle across the floor and out the door. For the first time I was aware of the rapt audience in the bar that had been watching the drama unfold. Kathy did up a couple of buttons.

"I rather liked them the way they were," I said.

"Did you really see Doolittle driving that truck?" Kathy asked.

"No. Just a guess. And there weren't any prints either. And where did your friends come from?"

"I called them from the ladies room. Told them to stand by outside the door."

"Okay—but do you usually carry handcuffs in your purse?"

"I'm a prostitute, remember. Tools of the trade."

I took her arm, and we walked through the bar like celebrities who had just won an Oscar. The last thing I heard was LeRoy calling out, "Everybody. Drinks on the house!"

34

I strolled across the Park, took a seat beside Number Six. I set his coffee down on the bench between us. Neither of us acknowledged the other's existence. KittyLuv was quiet; the limousine was not parked in front.

"Is the fucker in today?" I spoke to the trees. Six took the coffee and nodded. "Think I'll talk to him," I said.

I left Six on the bench, crossed Main Street, and walked down the ramp beside KittyLuv to the parking area in back. Many of the staff had not come to work, and there were only three cars in the lot. The black limousine was parked in front of the garage. There was no sign of Samson's battered pick-up truck. I walked up the stairs between the back of the building and the garage. The first landing had doors off both sides. On the right side the door to the downstairs file room was wide open. The door to the apartment over the garage was on the left. The label by the buzzer carried the name S. Wheatley. I was about to continue up to the back entrance to Lafonte's office when the apartment door opened.

"Looking for someone?" It was Samson.

The tone of his voice suggested to me that I should postpone the meeting. "No, just going up the back way." I turned to the stairs.

"Come in," Samson said.

"No thanks. I'm on my way."

"I said, come in!" The tenor of Samson's voice had changed. He was standing just inside the door. One hand was beckoning me to come inside; the other was holding a nasty-looking Baretta Cheetah. It was pointed at my mid-section, and at a distance of three feet his chances of hitting the target were pretty good. I accepted the invitation. Samson followed me down a short hallway and into his living room. It was a small, claustrophobic space. The curtains were closed and a couch, an overstuffed chair, and a large TV screen dominated the room. I felt the barrel of the pistol pushed into my back and stood still while Samson reached around and took my Glock from its shoulder holster. He backed up, reached behind him, and laid my pistol on the bookshelf at the end of the hall. "Sit!" Samson commanded, and pushed me toward the soft chair.

"I'd just as soon stand," I said. I realized that no one knew I was here. Samson seemed to be playing a game; tempting me to dive for my gun. I changed the subject. "Where'd you put the pick-up?"

"In the garage, dummy. Why do you care?" This time he pushed me into the chair with the barrel of his pistol in my gut. I sank into the cushions. There was no way to make a fast move from the womblike depths of the chair.

"You're toast," Samson sneered. "I've had enough of you. You know too damn much for your own good."

"You're not going to shoot me. There's no silencer on that piece of metal you're holding, the door to KittyLuv is wide open, and Rose is sitting ten feet inside." She wasn't, but it was worth a try. "You shoot me and the world knows it."

"I'll decide when to shoot you, punk."

Samson was enjoying his power, so I'd best just stall for time. Everyone wants to confess, or brag and get credit for the shit they pull. "So, Samson. Why did you do it?"

"Do what?"

"Kill Louella. You were sleeping with her for Christ's sake. Then you stabbed her. Why?"

Samson stared at me. "She didn't know her place."

"Yeah. She told me your cock was too small. She could hardly feel it inside her." I taunted him. It was a gamble, but maybe I could rile him into some crazy move. Guys don't want to shoot people who laugh at their tiny dick; they want to beat them up to prove it's not true. Samson stepped forward and swung the Baretta at my head. I blocked the swing with my left arm. Jesus! That hurt! I slumped back into the pillows, and felt a wetness growing on my left side. Damn pistol had opened up the stitches, and a circle of blood was growing on my jacket.

"Looks like your chair is about to get soaked with evidence," I challenged Samson.

He grabbed my collar with his left hand and jerked me up, out of the chair and onto the floor. The pistol in his right hand never lost its aim on my forehead. Samson grinned down at me. "You already shot one guy so I got self-defense on my side. You miserable shit! I'm going to enjoy putting a bullet in your brain."

I kept on. "You killed Louella to get that letter didn't you?"

"What letter are you talking about?"

"Chauffeurs listen in on a lot of stuff. You found out that Vera had that note when you heard her and Larry arguing over it, and you tried to get it from her."

"What do you know?" Samson sneered.

"I was there. Then you heard Louella fight with Larry in the limousine, and you realized that she had ended up with the letter. You heard her threaten to go to the papers unless he agreed to her demands."

"She wanted too much!"

"You'd do anything to keep her from destroying Larry."

"And why would I want to save Larry?"

"You tell me, *Sweetie*."

A heavy silence swept over the room. I looked up at Samson. Samson stared down at me. The iron jaw melted, and quivered. I thought he was about to cry.

"You love him, don't you," I pressed stubbornly on.

"You wouldn't understand. It wasn't just sex, he's, he's . . ." Samson stuttered.

"Like a father," I added.

"Yes! Like a father I never knew." He yelled at me. "Like a mother who died when I was born! Like a brother I never had! Like a lover! You wouldn't understand! Nobody would! And nobody's going to know! *Nobody!*"

Samson's face hardened back into concrete, and he raised the pistol. I was poised to make a desperate grab for his legs when he spun around toward the door. I saw the silhouette of a man, who stood still, stood without saying a word. Samson swung his gun toward the intruder and I grabbed Samson's leg and twisted. He reeled around and a shot fired into the ceiling, scattering chunks of plaster about the room. I yanked desperately on the leg, and Samson staggered and kept firing. Sharp bits of the shattered TV screen sprayed over us. Samson lashed out with his foot and caught me on the side of the head. Lightning bolts shot through my brain. I looked up to the steel barrel, inches from my face. A shot! Samson pitched over me and flattened against the couch. He was clutching his side with one hand and trying to aim at something with the pistol in the other. Another shot and I could see his chest collapse. His jaw fell open; his eyes stared ahead in disbelief, and then in death. Slowly the room came back into focus. The TV was shattered, the windows broken, the couch and floor stained with blood, and Number Six stood silently at the end of the hall, his right hand hanging by his side, my Glock pointed at the floor.

35

I struggled to my knees and then caught hold of the arm of the chair to help me stand up. I took two uneven steps forward and held out my hand. Number Six placed the Glock in my palm. I looked him in the eye. He looked at the floor. "Go! Quickly!" I ordered. He turned and slowly started back down the hall. I rubbed the handle of the Glock against my coat, dropped it into my pocket, and followed Six out the door. He started down the steps to the parking area, one step at a time, with his shifting slow gait. I ran up the stairs to Lafonte's terrace as fast as I could. I wanted to intercept anyone coming down to check on the gunshots before they could spot Six. I reached the terrace and fell up against the glass door. A scream cut through the air. Inside I saw Sybil—she had seen me, and her hand was covering her mouth as if she was facing a zombie. There was blood staining my jacket and dripping down the side of my head. Lafonte jumped up and was trying to open the glass door, but I leaned against it.

Six was moving slowly and was just leaving the bottom of the stairs. Rose was shouting something into Lafonte's phone. I had to give Six more time to get back to the Park. I slid down the door, leaving a trail of blood on the glass, and folded into a heap on the terrace. Lafonte stopped pushing on the door, he didn't want to slide me across the stones. I twisted my head up and tried to signal that I was okay, that I'd be on my feet in a moment. Lafonte yelled something to Sybil, and she raced out the office door to the hall. A minute later she appeared coming up the outside stairs—she had run through KittyLuv's ground floor to the back entrance to the landing below. She helped me away from the door, carefully keeping any blood off her dress. I quickly glanced down the stairs toward the parking lot; Number Six had finally disappeared around the corner.

Sybil was trying to make sense of the mess. "What happened? Are you okay?"

Before I could answer two figures rushed into the office, Kathy and JJ. JJ moved Lafonte aside and opened the door. Kathy ran through and caught me as I tipped over backwards. She pulled a tissue from her pocket and pressed it against my head, and held me tightly in her arms. More blue-coated officers burst into the office. There were far too many drawn pistols, pointing randomly at anything that moved.

"Kathy, how'd you get here?" My speech was slurred.

"Someone heard shots and called us. We raced over. Apparently too late."

The law had arrived too damn fast. Rose called them and they ran across the Park. Six didn't have time to get back to his bench; they had to have seen him shuffling away from the building.

"There's a dead guy in the apartment down there," I blurted out. "It's not pretty."

Lafonte heard me and tried to push through the door, but JJ held him back. "Is it Samson? Is he dead?" he shouted at me. He knew the answer. His face was a mask of despair. He held his head in his hands and sobbed, "Why? Why?"

I didn't want to say that Samson killed Lulu out of love for

Lafonte, but maybe Larry knew that already. Sybil came out of the office, took Lafonte's arm, and led him back inside. Kathy motioned to two officers and sent them down the stairs to the scene of the crime.

"Blue. What happened?" Kathy asked softly.

"Samson killed Louella. He did it to protect Larry Lafonte, his lover. He's Sweetie."

"He's Sweetie?" Kathy repeated, skeptically. "Lafonte and Samson were . . . ?" She didn't finish the thought.

"Yes. Look at his name. Samuel Wheatley. He signs his bar tabs 'S period Wheatley.' Sweetley. Sweetie."

"I'll be dammed." Kathy let the phrase slide between her teeth. "And you shot him?"

"Yes. He was crazy mad. He came after me and wanted to get rid of me next. He was shooting everything in sight."

Rose had brought a hand towel, and Kathy tied it around my head. Samson's foot had done some damage there. "Where's the gun?" she asked. I took the pistol out of my pocket, gripped it by the barrel, and slid it into the plastic evidence bag she held open. She handed it to JJ. The last thing I remember that day was a fascination with Kathy's uniform: it was covered with blood.

36

"You're lookin' pretty good, except for the sling. But it must be hard to get a hat on over that crazy bandage on your head." JJ met me at the door of the Police Headquarters. "How are things over at New Memorial Hospital?"

"Not bad, not bad. A couple of days rest was good for my soul. And Dr. Sanji—she adds a whole new chapter to the concept of bed rest."

"I won't ask," JJ said. "Let's go upstairs. Chief MacGregor would like to talk with you."

Kathy was at her desk. Four other cops were in the room. "Hey, look who's here!" Corbutt called out and came over to shake my hand.

Young Tom was also there—he referred to me in the third person. "He looks better than those pictures in the papers."

Kathy interrupted the merrymaking. "Okay, guys. Enough of the plaudits. You've got better things to do. JJ, you stick around."

"Yes sir, Chief." Corbutt saluted and led the crew out.

JJ and I sat opposite Kathy. She leafed through a folder labeled "KittyLuv Case One." We were waiting to see where she wanted to start.

"He was in plain sight, he was out of sight." Kathy shook her head. '*Sweetie*' doesn't bring up an image of a six-foot-something macho guy wearing a chauffeur's uniform and we couldn't see him." Kathy looked at me. "S period Wheatley. Sweetley. You could have told us and saved yourself a lot of trouble."

"I wasn't sure. I thought I'd go find out. Didn't think he would get all in my face with that 'I'm-going-to-shoot-you' stuff."

"We've been looking into Wheatley. There's pretty good evidence that he was having an affair with Mrs. Lafonte. The garden crew recognized his photo. We have a DNA match between some hairs we took from Mrs. Lafonte's nails, and Wheatley's, and there's some of her blood on the steering wheel of his pick-up. It's circumstantial, but it's pretty strong."

"He was driven by a passion," I added. "I doubt there was much premeditation in anything he did."

"Also," Kathy went on, "the DA seems satisfied with your description of the fight with Wheatley, particularly since he can't come up with any other explanation."

"Not bad for a guy who shot two people in a week," JJ chipped in.

"He's a bit skeptical, though, but he can't find anyone else to pin it on." Kathy looked me in the eye.

"Unless the killer was wearing that helmet you were talking about, and became invisible." JJ chuckled.

Kathy turned to another page of the file. "As for Calibano . . ."

"Knockout, " I corrected her.

"The dirt on Knockout is coming out. Doolittle is savoring his role as a diva. He's singing like he's starring in *Tosca*. He admits to telling Jones that Alexander was coming down to test for lead in the soil, and he's doing everything he can to pin it all on Jones."

JJ added, "That's a court case that will drag on for a while. It's Doolittle's word versus Jones. Jones may get off on the murder charge, but I'm sure he'll get something. And Hope Estates is a thing of the past."

"What about Lafonte?" I asked.

"He should stay out of jail," Kathy explained. "Your finance guy, Henry Cadman, is working with him to sell off his estate and repay the loan. Cadman has already put the books under a microscope, and I have to admit, Blue, you were right. It looks like they were running a legitimate operation—they actually just want to help homeless cats. Jones had no way to blackmail Lafonte into buying the Factory until Doolittle told him about the shady loan."

"The loan was his Achilles paw. He had to choose between losing KittyLuv by protecting his goddaughter or buying the Factory for Jones and selling Vera out. A no-win situation."

"Lafonte has resigned, but KittyLuv will probably survive, although in a slightly reduced form. The accountant, Miss Davidson, is taking over as interim president."

"Thalia." I said. "Good choice. She won't take any crap from the press."

I was having trouble keeping up with the details. My head hurt, Samson had given it a solid kick, and shooting people left me with a bunch of metaphysical questions. "And Vera?" I asked.

"Vera." Kathy laughed. "She's unstoppable. She's going ahead with The Bishop Museum for Old and Really Cool Machines, or something like that. And you know what?"

"What?"

"She's bringing in the one and only Larry Lafonte to head up the Museum."

"Wow!" was all my addled brain could come up with.

JJ saw an opening. "Sounds like I'm done here. Got to get back to work."

Kathy gave him the okay; JJ winked at me and closed the door on his way out.

Kathy turned to me. "Tell me more about Wheatley. He seemed like such a ladies' man."

"Yes, but that was just sex," I explained.

"Just sex?" Kathy looked at me with a puzzled expression.

"Yes. He killed for all the other things—love, trust, devotion. He'd do anything to protect his lover, although I can't say he thought it through very well."

"Just sex? You're saying that if he just stuck with sex he'd have stayed out of trouble? Sounds like some kind of justification for your lifestyle."

"Yep. And if I can't have you I've decided to give up sex, or maybe I'll give up martinis, or both."

Kathy laughed again. "How about you take me to dinner tonight after work and we can let food enter into the equation. Doolittle derailed our last date."

"Sounds good. A couple of martinis, nice rare steak, and . . ."

"And some good conversation," Kathy prompted.

"Conversation?"

"Blue, I have a lot of questions."

"About Samson?"

"No. About the weather, about you and me, about what you're hiding from." Kathy waited while I rolled the questions over in my mind.

"Okay. I'll leave the helmet with Javier at the Arms. A few of my neighbors could use it. But . . ."

"But, what?"

"But you have to wear that sexy dress again, with the low neckline."

"It's a deal, and I'll put you in charge of the buttons." Kathy smiled. "Now I've got a lot of work to do to wrap up all these bodies you've left lying around."

. . . .

Number Six was sitting on his bench on the other side of the Park. I picked up two coffees, walked over, and sat down next to him. Six didn't look my way, or say anything. I understood what he did. He hated Samson. Samson had chased Vera—I told him that—and Samson tried to throw him off his bench. He had watched me head for a showdown with Samson. Number Six came down to check on me.

Number Six held out his hand. For a moment I thought he wanted to shake but then realized he just wanted the coffee. "Thanks, Six," I said, and handed him the paper cup. He said nothing, and we sat silently on the bench. The workday was ending—a steady stream of tired workers were filing out and spreading loosely in all directions. The shadow of the red oak crept toward the bench. Summer was thinking about retirement, and the days were beginning to shorten. A breeze from the north was cool enough to bring on a slight shiver. I was about to try again to thank Six and tell him Vera was fine when he turned away from me. I was looking at his back and he was watching the workers file out of the Hamilton Office Building. Then I saw the light. A glowing light was moving along the sidewalk. A blond head, billows of hair reflecting the low afternoon sunlight. The ball of fire floated by the Park until it was extinguished as she turned the corner. The Doctor's receptionist, June, had entered into Six's mind, and he was transfixed.

Number Six slowly rose from his seat. He said nothing and started his slow journey home—or wherever he went at night. I watched him walk, empty coffee cup in hand, to the end of the Park. He stopped by a trash basket. Studied it for a moment, then threw his cup on the ground and shuffled out of sight into the shadow beside the County Courthouse.

Kathy wouldn't be leaving work for another hour, so the bench seemed a good place to hang out. I felt something rub against my leg.

"Cat-Meow. How are you?" He answered that he was fine. I picked him up, settled him on my lap, and scratched him behind the ears. He purred. Cat-Meow and Six knew the secrets of contentment. Number Six had become invisible. Half the town's police force had raced by him and never saw him. He had reversed the idiom. He wasn't seen as a person any more. He no longer existed in the mind of our town. Out Of Mind, out of sight.

The shadow cast by the grand oak tree moved slowly. When it covers me, it will be time to wander over to LeRoy's to meet Kathy.

I slid over to Six's side of the bench.

About the Author

Michael Burke has traveled through a number of careers since he graduated from college. The first was as an astronomer, working at observatories in the U.S., Hawaii, and Iran. He then went back to school to obtain a Master's Degree in City Planning. He worked in New York City's Planning Department and later became an Assistant Professor at Columbia's Graduate School of Architecture and City Planning. Michael changed direction again when he found a loft in Soho and began to paint. He has been an artist for more than thirty years—painting, drawing, and lately producing aluminum books and sculpture. He has exhibited his work extensively in the U.S., Japan, and Europe. Although he has written and published poetry over the years, Michael has only recently arrived on the mystery scene. *Swan Dive* was published in 2009 and *Music of the Spheres* in 2011. *Out of Mind*, the further adventures of detective Johnny "Blue" Heron, is the third book in the series.

MICHAEL BURKE

About the Author

Michael Burke has traveled through a number of careers since he graduated from college. The first was as an astronomer, working at observatories in the U.S., Hawaii, and Iran. He then went back to school to obtain a Master's Degree in City Planning. He worked in New York City's Planning Department and later became an Assistant Professor at Columbia's Graduate School of Architecture and City Planning. Michael changed direction again when he found a loft in Soho and began to paint. He has been an artist for more than thirty years—painting, drawing, and lately producing aluminum books and sculpture. He has exhibited his work extensively in the U.S., Japan, and Europe. Although he has written and published poetry over the years, Michael has only recently arrived on the mystery scene. *Swan Dive* was published in 2009 and *Music of the Spheres* in 2011. *Out of Mind*, the further adventures of detective Johnny "Blue" Heron, is the third book in the series.

MICHAEL BURKE

www.ingramcontent.com/pod-product-compliance
Lightning Source LLC
Chambersburg PA
CBHW020650260626
47157CB00008B/2980